JOHNSTOWN

A NOVEL BY
ROBERT WHITMORE
COPYRIGHT 2024

Chapter 1

"We did it!" Jack Westchester shouted as he watched the election results tick by while Channel 4 reporter Heather Marie talked about the regional results. "I'm the mayor of Johnstown!"

Dozens of supporters had come to Jack's house to watch the results come in. They had spent many nights and weekends helping him with door-to-door canvassing and mailing. So, staying up past midnight to see who won seemed reasonable. Most of them were drunk, thanks to a generous open bar set up in the kitchen.

"Fifty-six votes isn't much of a margin," Rhett Tanner said, as he joined Jack. He sipped a beer and considered the last twelve months, when he had served as campaign manager for the new mayor.

"I'm confident it will be enough," Jack said. "We pitted the other two against each other and went with the grassroots approach. A fine idea on your part."

"It was an easy approach. You are the descendant of the city's founder and focused on your personal side instead of promising deals to corporations. I'd say one of them might ask for a recount."

"Melissa Stevens will settle back in as president of the city council. She still has plenty of power there and won't want to risk her connections by stirring the pot."

"And Will Irmler?"

"Oh, I think the plans he has to expand his factory might be helped along with a phone call from the mayor. I should call him."

"Not wasting any time," Rhett said and took a long drink. "That's why I'm in your camp."

"And I'm glad you are," Jack said. He looked around and saw that everyone was enjoying their own conversations. "My plans for the old homeplace will finally get out of deadlock. Preserving my family history in Johnstown is something I really want, and it will serve me well when I run for re-election. Melissa will be less likely to have her little trio of council members block me and I can start calling in official favors from Jefferson City. Officially, I'm just the hometown boy who is working for the people. My friends will certainly be rewarded sooner than later. That includes you."

"You've paid me well to do this."

"I'll worry about what extra you deserve. Call it a bonus for the win."

"You're the boss, Mr. Mayor," Rhett said.

"Yes. Yes, I am."

Six months later, Jack had managed to remove all the red tape around the John Westchester Homestead project. That old house had been Jack's inheritance and the acreage it sat on would soon be his big payday. A major bank had been attempting to secure land in that part of Johnstown for a decade and they were willing to pay handsomely.

To clear the way for his project, he agreed to preserve the house and allow for extra oversight to win over the Missouri State Historical Society. As mayor, he had convinced the planning commission that the new bank project would be a good use for the land by getting the bank to submit new plans for the structure that would contribute more to the aesthetics of Johnstown. His final triumph had been winning over the city council by agreeing to donate a forty acre tract he owned in the west part of town to the city's recreation department. He had hoped it would be a high-priced new subdivision someday, but it would become a park instead.

This new park would be exactly what Melissa Stevens had promised to work on during her last campaign. A pond, tennis cour222ts, jogging path, and three pavilions would be in the first phase of the park. It would also be the new home of the house that city founder John Westchester had once lived in.

All these things were swimming through Jack's mind when the gravel along the edge of Ballpark Drive began to pop and crack. He had driven to this spot so many times that his city issued, white pickup practically drove itself there, although it was only a quarter of a mile from city hall.

The emblem of the City of Johnstown covered most of the truck's front doors. It had been his request to have the emblem put on, so that people would be more aware of his presence among the people of Johnstown. Working for the people is what would secure his re-election in four years.

This trip was personal, but he still used the truck. Jack put it in park, sat back, and smiled. He was looking toward the crew of construction workers bustling around a small, yellow house at the top of a short rise. John Westchester's house.

"Good things do come to those who wait," he said to himself before looking in the mirror on the back of his visor. He inspected his gelled black hair, wanting to make sure that each strand was in its place. His bright blue eyes twinkled as he thought about how great his day was going to be. "Or maybe God helps those who help themselves is more appropriate for me."

Jack got out of his truck and put on his golden hardhat, being sure not to disturb his hair any more than necessary. He looked like a millionaire investor and that was exactly what he wanted to be. He walked at a slow and deliberate pace, stopping to observe the construction equipment that was moving about the property. This land had been in his family for two centuries, but now this equipment was helping to send it on to its next owner.

He was also pleased to see a semi with a long flatbed trailer bearing 'Wide Load' signs sitting along Westchester Road in front of the house, blocking one lane of traffic. Each piece of equipment was yellow and had the name Freemantle painted on the side. He had heard good things about this company and so he paid extra to bring them in from Minnesota. Getting the house to its new location was critical.

Jack took his time walking up the gentle slope and across what had been the lawn of the small house. He wanted everyone to see him, but stopped ten feet from two men who were studying some plans, waiting to be greeted. Each of the workers at the site had white hardhats, except one. He wore a black hardhat and was the first to acknowledge the mayor's arrival.

"Good morning, Mayor Westchester!" said the man in the black hat as he walked away from the worker holding the plans.

"Good morning, Mr. Kelly," the mayor said. "I insist that you call me Jack, though."

"Then you will have to call me Bill," he said. He offered his best attempt to match the mayor's joy and shook his hand.

"That's a deal," Jack replied. "Now, how are things looking today? The weather seems perfect for the move."

"I agree and we should be on our way by mid-afternoon. Definitely before traffic picks up around four-thirty."

"That is excellent news. It is a great day for Johnstown. This area was purchased by my family a long time ago. John Westchester had big dreams and those dreams have been realized in the last few decades. Johnstown is growing. He would be proud and would be glad to know his home place will be getting a much better location."

"Pretty amazing that you got the deal done to move the house," Bill said. "State Historical Site and all the paperwork that goes with it."

"Well," Jack said with a wink, "it took a lot of phone calls, and I did some good negotiating. Lots of favors and promises in Jefferson City and the city council demanded that I set aside land for the house to be relocated on."

"Progress!" Bill said. "Congratulations, Jack."

"Yes, it certainly is, and thank you. This property has been in demand for a long time and now the deal is nearly done. Fifteen acres along one of the busiest thoroughfares in western San Luis

County is unheard of these days. Missouri National Bank made an offer that I, as the head of Westchester Holdings, could not reject."

"That's awesome," Bill said, hoping that the conversation was over. It wasn't.

"New Johnstown Park will be a great place to display the home and the bank gets a fantastic new branch. Johnstown wins all around," Jack said, thinking of the fact that he would be two million dollars richer as soon as the bank took ownership of the property.

"Things are going smoothly today. We just need to put four more beams in place to lift the house and bring the crane in. After that, we will put the house on the truck and be on our way. The new foundation over at the park is ready, so the house should be resting peacefully by nightfall."

"Wonderful," Jack said. "Mind if I hang around for a bit?"

"Sure thing. The crane will be here in an hour if you want to see that process."

"I've got a meeting about that time, but I'll watch them put the beams in."

"Enjoy. I'm going to get back to work," Bill said, and Jack nodded. They shook hands before Bill walked away.

Jack made his way over to two men looking over the construction plans, which were tacked to a piece of plywood on a pair of sawhorses. They gave every appearance that things were going as predicted. One of the men, Tony DiPietri, was gesturing toward the porch at the back of the house, where three more beams were lined up. Putting those in place and then connecting the beams so that the crane could pick the house up was all that remained.

Jack watched them for a moment and walked over to a yellow truck with the name Freemantle painted on it. He believed he was in charge of everything, including other people's vehicles. So, he opened the passenger door, dusted off the already spotless seat, and sat down. He watched the workers shuffling around, but he only saw them as pawns moving him closer to making his fortune.

"Less than a month," he said to himself as he pulled his iPhone from the pocket of his shirt that had been pressed the day before. He began scrolling through a list of emails as he waited.

Ten minutes later, the crew had lined up the last three beams on the ground next to the porch. One man was crawling underneath with a steel cable in tow. A Bobcat waited on the other side to pull the beam, while a backhoe pushed. The revving of engines brought Jack's attention back to the task at hand.

"Let's go!" Bill yelled into his radio and the cable under the porch went taut.

The backhoe started pushing with its bucket and the beam slid smoothly under the porch, leaving about three inches to spare. Bill felt relief as they neared completion. He signaled to the backhoe operator, who moved to the next beam.

Minutes later, the worker scrambled back under the house with the cable to prepare the next placement. Jack noticed that others were busy bolting the beams under the main part of the house together. Everything was going well, and he hadn't stopped smiling. He imagined what he was going to do with his first wave of purchases as a millionaire.

"Two to go!" Bill called into his radio and the process started again. The beam slipped along until there was a hollow thud and the beam suddenly jumped. A loud crack like thunder came from under the house and Bill started waving his hands. The backhoe stopped immediately, and the cable went slack a moment later.

"What was that?" the backhoe driver yelled as he killed the engine on his machine.

Bill didn't like getting his information second hand, so he rushed to the side of the house and got down on his hands and knees to take a look. He could see the beam wedged between a thick stone and one of the floor joists, which had a bad break in it.

"Shit," he said under his breath and started crawling under the porch. The man who had pulled the cable through was close behind him. Tony joined them.

"Damn," he said, looking at the broken joist.

"How did this happen, Tony?" Bill asked in an angry tone, while doing his best to stay calm. He scooped up some loose dirt in his hand from next to the stone and shook his head.

"I don't know," Tony replied. "I came through here three times and found nothing but dirt. It looks like the beam found a soft spot, dug in, and hit that stone."

"That has to be a pretty heavy stone to deflect the beam. Don't you think?"

"Definitely, but there was nothing on the plans or in the house's history to indicate anything like that under the porch."

"Get some guys under here and frame up that damage. The mayor is watching, and I don't want any more hiccups. Also, figure out what that stone is. Pull it out before pushing that beam under again. With our luck, someone from the historical society will be here to shut us down if they hear about this. Let's move quickly."

"You got it, boss," Tony said and started inspecting the damage.

Within minutes, two more men were scrambling under the house with two by sixes and nail guns. Tony had grabbed a small shovel from the toolbox on the side of the Bobcat and gone straight back under the house to inspect the stone. Seeing the commotion, Jack left the truck and walked over to the porch to get a better look. His confidence gave way to concern that the plan was in jeopardy.

"Is there a problem, Bill?" Jack asked.

"I don't think so," Bill answered, standing up to face the mayor. "One of the floor joists was damaged, but they will have it braced up in a minute. We will still be moving the house today. Tony is looking into what caused this."

"That's good to hear. I'm going to head over to my meeting, but make sure you text me when you get the house on the truck."

"I will certainly do that."

"Great!" the mayor said before turning to walk back to his vehicle.

Bill watched the mayor go and was relieved when the city truck pulled away. He was not afraid of angering the mayor, but he also did not like being micromanaged. He heard a shuffle under the edge of the porch and turned his attention back to where Tony was coming out.

"What did you find?"

"It's a pretty big stone. It's round and it appears to be sitting on top of bricks. It reminds me of the well cap that was at my grandparent's farm when I was a kid. I'm hoping it isn't hiding something that wasn't on the plans. The beam cracked it."

"Can we get the house off with that stone where it is?"

"Probably, but I think we should put a chain around it and get it out of there. The construction crew won't want to deal with it when they start on the bank."

"That works for me," Bill said. "Let's get this thing going."

"I'll have the guys dig out more so that we don't come across any more surprises."

"Sounds great," Bill said and walked back to the piece of plywood holding the site plans. Having a well under the house was unusual, but the porch could have been a kitchen at some point. He hoped it would be nothing more than a bump in the road.

Tony went back under the house and continued to dig, creating a sort of ramp in the dirt. He hoped the stone would slide out easily and they could get this project behind them. A heavy chain was fit into the trench that the others had dug around the large stone. Although the stone had been partially split by the beam, he hoped that it would come out in one piece.

"Take it slow," Bill said as the backhoe started backing up a minute later. The slack went out of the chain and the tires gave a brief spin, but then got a good grip. The engine roared as it crept along in reverse at a cautious pace. Bill's frown faded as the dirt packed old stone slid out from under the house.

"That's beautiful," Tony said as the trailing edge cleared the house.

"Stop!" Bill ordered and waved his gloved right hand to the backhoe driver.

Tony pumped his fist in celebration but then gave two hard coughs. He stumbled away from the house and then went down to one knee. Bill rushed toward him, but stopped short when a severe coughing fit took him, too. The air smelled rancid, like a big sewer rat had died in stagnant water before being sealed up for a year.

Two other workers ran over to them. Both would later swear that they saw grayish green smoke roll out from under the house. Bill and Tony each regained their breath after a minute. One of the workers brought them each a bottle of water, which helped. The coughing fit passed as quickly as it had started.

"I want to see this done today," Bill said, twisting the cap back onto his empty bottle and tossing it in a black trash barrel two feet away.

"I'm with you on that," Tony replied, following Bill's lead.

The crew put in the last two beams and started bolting them all together. When they finished, it would be like a large steel mesh to lift the entire house. Jack had secured the necessary permits for them to move the house on one truck instead of having to split it, which was frowned upon by representatives of the historical society.

"What was that?" Tony asked Bill in a quiet tone once they had gotten away from the other workers.

"It was disgusting," Bill said, faking a gag. "I bet that well or cistern or whatever it is has been sealed up for more than a hundred and fifty years."

"Yeah, who knows what's down there?"

"Nothing. We really need there to be nothing down there that could set this project back."

"Right, I meant that maybe some dumb animal had burrowed in there and died."

"Let's make sure one of us is the first to investigate once the house is gone."

"You got it," Tony said, going off to supervise the workers bolting the beams together.

The pounding of pneumatic impact drivers echoed off the shopping center across the street. About that time, four men in a red SuperCrew Ford truck had pulled into the parking lot at the Johnstown Methodist Church. The church was at the east side of the construction site and provided a great spot to watch the proceedings. Each was sipping coffee from QuikTrip.

"Never seen anything like this. How about you, Bob?" Leon Irvon asked, gesturing his cup toward the house.

"Nope," Bob Glenn replied. "They used to just tear these things down and put a picture in a museum. What do you think about this whole thing, Dean?"

"Well, I guess someone is bound to make money off of this," Dean Burl said, taking a long drink from his cup.

"That's a fact," Jimmy Charles commented. "I was down at Uncle Bill's yesterday and talked to two of the guys on the zoning board. The mayor stands to make better than two million bucks on this."

"Two million?" Dean exclaimed. "Then why is the city involved?"

"Now, now," Jimmy said. "We all know how these things work. The historical society doesn't want you to move their designated buildings, but enough money in the right places will get anything done. Oftentimes, those channels have to be through a municipality."

"Right," Leon said, with a laugh. "All for the betterment of Johnstown."

"Sure, it is," Bob said sarcastically. "We definitely need another bank along Westchester Avenue. I can only see four from here."

"It's the free market at work," Jimmy stated in an equally sarcastic tone. "If we want to see the old place, we only have to drive over to that fancy new park."

"I suppose the mayor is paying for that new park himself. Seeing as he's the one making the profit?" Dean asked.

"I'm sure," Bob said after a long drink of black coffee. "Too bad Gerald couldn't be here to see this today."

The men fell silent, focusing on the workers and thinking about what they would do with two million dollars. The truck carrying the crane had arrived and was being unloaded on the north side of the house. Traffic had begun to slow with people trying to catch a glimpse as they went by on Westchester Avenue.

The beams under the house were all secured with a crisscross of cables and smaller beams. They had begun fastening together the thick cables that would be used to lift the house. The four men were still watching as the crane swung its massive arm over the house with about twenty of the thick cables hanging down. Each one had a worker with a rope on the other end, making sure the cables did not damage or even touch the house.

Bob and his crew of friends drove back over to Quik Trip for a refill on coffee and a bathroom break, but they wasted no time getting back to the church parking lot. They did not want to miss a moment of the house moving. Two cars and another truck had joined them for the show.

"How long do you think it'll actually take?" Leon asked as soon as Bob shut off the engine.

"I'd say thirty minutes," Dean said. "I guess it depends how fast that crane can move it over to the truck."

"Here we go!" Jimmy said with excitement from the back seat, as the crane lifted the beams up.

The steel pressed gently against the bottom of the house and then the crane operator revved the engine to start applying more pressure. The men in the truck, most of the workers, Tony, and Bill all watched and waited. Bill had his phone out, ready to text the mayor. Two men with sledgehammers were at each footing for the house, ready to break the stone loose if the foundation didn't come apart on its own. Luckily, there were no problems, and the house drifted up from the spot it had occupied for over a hundred years.

"We did it, boss," Tony said, walking up to stand next to Bill.

"I'll be happy when it is actually in the park, but this is a good start."

Men with ropes tied to the beams were walking alongside the house as the crane crawled toward the road. Their job was to make sure the house did not twist or hit anything along the way. They would also be sure the house was placed squarely on the flatbed of the tractor trailer.

More drivers on Westchester Avenue were slowing to gawk at the floating house. With one of the two west-bound lanes already closed, traffic started to back up. Even at three in the afternoon, that stretch of road could get busy in a hurry. It became clear that for each interested person, there was one who was not interested in watching and simply wanted to be on their way. Tempers flared and drivers started yelling. They honked their horns at those who had slowed to watch.

"Tony, get down there and tell those people they need to move along," Bill said. "This is going to take a while longer and we don't want to give the mayor any more reasons to get upset."

"Sure," Tony said, immediately jogging down to the edge of the road. He took a spot behind the flatbed that would haul the house, but still inside the orange cones that had been set up. He started waving his arms, encouraging traffic to continue on its way. "Keep moving please! Pull off on Ballpark if you want to watch!"

Traffic started moving quicker and cars pulled off onto a side road. Two of the irate drivers slowed to give Tony their opinion on the whole thing before speeding away. A silver Jeep Liberty came flying in toward him in the right lane, cutting over into the left lane at the last second, forcing an older woman in a burgundy Buick to slam on her brakes. He threw his hands in the air and his heart skipped a beat, but he froze instead of jumping out of the way.

"Get out of the road, asshole!" the woman in the Liberty yelled as she sped off.

"Some people just need to relax," Tony said to himself, trying to calm down, as he continued waving cars through.

Chapter 2

"Hey, Patty, it's Marsha," said Marsha Benton through her hands free speaker as she cruised west along Westchester Avenue in her silver Liberty.

"What's up, Marsh? Are you off work already?"

"Yeah, I took the afternoon off to run errands. I had to go to the store to buy groceries for tonight and pick up things for around the house. You *are* still coming, right?"

"Absolutely," Patty replied. "Charlie and Amanda will be there, too."

"Great. It has been way too long since we all got together and..."

"And?" Patty asked.

"Ugh, I hate Westchester. This road is always backed up for one reason or another. I'm just trying to have a good finish to my day after Bill chewed me out for not putting the new cover sheet on a report I turned in. Same information, but apparently, he has time to redesign a stupid cover sheet. The customers don't even see it! Ridiculous. Then I had an asthma attack. It is the single worst feeling in the world to not be able to breathe right."

"I'm glad you got it under control," Patty offered. "Just think about how much fun we are going to have tonight and I'm betting you got something delicious for us to enjoy."

"Definitely. I'm going to grill out steaks and bake some potatoes. Spinach salad and brownies with ice cream for dessert. The kid at the store was basically useless. He didn't know where anything was, and I probably lost ten minutes wandering around looking for stuff."

"You want me to come over early and help out?"

"No, I'm just having a rough day. Getting home sometime in the next hour would be nice. It looks like there is some sort of construction up ahead. Cars are stopped. Great."

"Aren't they moving that house today?" Patty asked.

"I forgot all about that," Marsha said, smacking her hand against the steering wheel. "Yep, the right lane looks closed. I should've gone a different way. This ice cream better not melt. Oh, I see an opening."

Marsha stomped on the gas and shot forward along the right lane, which was blocked with orange cones less than half a block ahead. A worker was behind the cones, waving his hands for her to get over, but she saw a burgundy Buick Regal creeping along three car lengths in front of her. She knew she could jump the line if she could get in front of that car before she got to the cones.

Seconds later, she hit the brakes and swerved to the left. She barely missed the front bumper of the Regal but managed to squeeze her Liberty into the spot. The worker threw his hands in the air with a shocked look on his face and she glared back at him, looking none too pleased that they were blocking the road.

"Get out of the road, asshole!" she yelled.

"What? Everything ok?" Patty asked.

"Yeah, I had to do some fancy driving. Anyway, I'm only a minute from home and I need to call my mom before I get there. She'll want to talk for an hour, but I can tell her I have to get out of the car. That always works."

"Okay then," Patty said with a laugh. "I'll talk to you tonight around seven."

"I'll be ready!"

"Catch you later, alligator."

"You're so weird," Marsha said and ended the call.

She sped along Westchester for another mile, moving from lane to lane to avoid people who had the gall to drive somewhere near the speed limit. She was pleased to catch a yellow left turn arrow at Old Johnstown Road and nearly took it on two wheels. The speed limit was thirty, but she hit fifty as she raced up the first hill.

She topped it and had to slam on her brakes, swerving left to avoid an old white Taurus that had stopped for a crossing guard near Johnstown Middle School. Her heart was in her throat as she came to a stop just shy of the crosswalk. The crossing guard bear hugged the student in front of her. A look of shock turned to anger as she glared at Marsha.

Once they cleared the crosswalk, she went ahead of the other cars to get back in the correct lane.

"What the hell are you doing, Marsha? You gotta calm down," she said to herself. "No, it's ok. I'm not used to coming through here during school time. An easy mistake to make. No big deal."

A half mile later, she slowed to turn into her subdivision. Her street was only a hundred feet beyond the edge of the new park, and she started thinking about how convenient it was going to be once it was done. She signaled her turn and glanced in the rearview at the park. She had been making that turn for over ten years, so it was automatic.

Still looking in the rearview mirror, she let off the accelerator, knowing that the turn was just ahead. Her eyes snapped from the mirror back to the road in front of her and she once again found herself stomping on the brakes. A man in a neon green hoodie and black shorts was running through the crosswalk, but was trying to stop himself as he saw the Jeep turning in. He slapped the side of her Jeep as she rolled by and flipped her off.

"Watch where you're going!" he yelled, once he saw that she had stopped and was looking back at him.

"You should look twice, you idiot!" Marsha called back.

"I hope you crash!" he yelled and took off running toward the new park.

"Well, I hope you actually DO get hit by a car!" Marsha answered. "Some people are ridiculous. If I wasn't in such a hurry,

I'd follow him and tell him exactly what I think about people who just assume they have the right of way in a crosswalk."

Her adrenaline was pumping as she continued down her street, going slower now. Cars were parked at random intervals along the left and right side of the street, so she had to maneuver carefully along the road she always insisted was too narrow. Three gentle curves and two small hills were the only real obstacles she had to overcome to finish her journey home.

As she pulled into the driveway, she clicked the remote to open the garage door. She had made a mental list of things she wanted to get done before her guests arrived and she was finally willing to admit she was feeling stressed out. Not all of those things would get done.

Cleaning the guest bathroom and sweeping all the leaves off the deck were the highest priority, but she also wanted to make sure the stainless steel grill was spotless. She was proud of it and considered it the centerpiece of her deck. That would have to wait until she could get the groceries taken in the house and put away.

Marsha shut off the engine, clicked the button to close the garage door behind her, and slipped her cell phone into her back left pants pocket. The bags with ice cream and other frozen desserts were in the passenger seat next to her, so she took them first. Although the door from the garage to the house was not accessible from outside, she kept it locked. She cursed herself this time because her hands were full, and she had already put her keys away.

Once she had put the first few bags on the counter, she glanced down at her FitBit. She saw that she still needed three thousand steps to reach her goal, so she made extra trips to the car instead of her normal plan of carrying as many bags as she could lift. She also knew that time was short, so she picked up her pace.

The vegetables and meat made it in on the second and third trips. She was thinking ahead to her chores when she opened the door to the garage the last time. She went down the steps into the garage and froze.

Standing near the wall on the far side of the garage was a man.

"Hey! How did you get in here? Get out!"

The man had his head down with his arms hanging at his side. She could not see his face and his absolute stillness gave her an even greater sense of unease. Then, she recognized his outfit, which was a green hoodie with black shorts.

"Listen here!" she yelled at him. "If you have a problem with me, that's fine. You can't just come on private property. Get out, right now!"

Still, the man did not respond, and she started to back up the stairs. She did not want to take her eyes off of him, so she searched blindly for the door frame with her right hand. Her left hand was reaching back to grab her cell phone.

"Get out!" she yelled again, the fear becoming evident in her voice for the first time. She grasped the edge of her phone and pulled it out in front of her. "I'll call the police!"

Her heel struck the edge of the step and she had to balance herself against the door frame. In that instant, the man crossed the garage, although she never saw his legs move. His right hand snapped up and grabbed her by the throat, lifting slightly. She swallowed hard as his grip tightened and she took a deep breath, planning to let out the loudest scream of her life.

Before she could do that, though, his hand squeezed with inhuman strength and closed off her airway. His thumb was pressed hard into her throat, and she looked up at his face for the first time. There was no expression on his face, not anger or even the slightest sign of effort as she struggled against him.

Then, she saw his eyes. They were solid black. Not just the irises, but the whole eyeball. She reached up with her right hand and dug her nails into his left, which he had used to completely encircle her neck.

Panic overtook her. Her mouth moved, but no sound came out. She felt the faintness wash over her as the black eyes stared down at her. With one final swipe of her right hand, she struck him in the face, but it had no effect. She continued trying to fight him, but each swing was weaker than the last. Her kicks had no effect, as the thing stared back at her. Finally, it gave a solid squeeze and crushed her throat.

Patty pulled into Marsha's driveway about four hours later. Charlie and Amanda were already there and were standing on the front porch. Patty saw they were each holding a bottle of wine and got hers from the seat next to her. She was smiling to herself, thinking of the craziness that was sure to ensue.

"You two didn't have to wait for me to go in!" Patty said with a laugh.

"Oh, well, we didn't want to spoil your arrival," Charlie said. "But really, we rang the doorbell, and she didn't answer."

"Really? I bet she's taking a shower or something. She sounded pretty stressed when I talked to her earlier."

"We haven't been here long, though," Amanda said. "No big deal."

"Right, but I'm ready to get this party started! I'll call her," Patty said. She set her bottle down on the porch and pulled her phone from the side pocket of her purse. She typed in her code and tapped the phone icon. Marsha was in the recent calls list, and she tapped her name.

The phone started ringing, but thirty seconds later it went to voicemail. Marsha's chipper voice told her to leave a message and that she would get back to her as soon as she could.

"Hello!" Patty said into the phone. "You have guests waiting outside. We don't care if you have your makeup on. We have wine! Open the door."

She ended the call and waited for a moment for a response. She then sent a text and started peeking in through the living room window but saw nothing unusual. The only light she could see was coming from the kitchen, although she couldn't see into that room.

"I'm going to walk around back and see if she's in the kitchen or outside," Patty said to the others.

"Sounds good," Amanda said. "We'll wait here in case she comes to the front door."

"Okay," Patty said, feeling uneasy. She dialed the phone as she walked back across the front of the house, going toward the sidewalk next to the garage that led to the backyard.

She was close to the corner when a sound stopped her in her tracks. She could hear the phone ringing on her end, but she also heard the ever familiar 'Who Can It Be Now?' ringtone that Marsha used. The song was coming from somewhere inside the house. She held her phone away from her ear to make sure she was not imagining it.

"What's wrong?" Charlie asked after seeing Patty stop.

"I can hear it ringing, but can't tell where it's coming from," she answered, rushing back over to the porch. She stooped to pick up a small decorative stone and revealed a blue, plastic box about the size of a book of matches. She flipped open the lid and took out a brass colored key with a red rubber grip on it. She dropped the little box and went to the front door. Seconds later, she walked into the house.

"Marsha!" she yelled, moving toward the kitchen. "Where are you?"

"Marsha?" Charlie called up the stairs, but the second floor was dark.

Patty stepped into the kitchen and saw a row of plastic grocery sacks on the counter. She saw ice cream in the first one and could tell it had been sitting out for a while. She glanced around and noticed that everything looked normal. Then, she saw that the back door was slightly ajar and knew that was not right. Marsha always kept her doors closed and locked.

"Marsha?" Patty called softly as she pulled the door open. The light was on in the garage, and she could see her friend sprawled out in front of her across the concrete floor. One foot was still on the step and her cell phone was about four feet away from her outstretched hand. Her eyes bulged from their sockets and looked up at her. Blood had run down her left cheek and dried on the floor after her head hit the ground. She stared at the black and purple handprints on Marsha's neck.

Patty screamed. Charlie and Amanda came running. Charlie saw Marsha's body, pulled the phone from his pocket, and dialed 911.

About a mile away, Josh Lanahan was throwing his running clothes into the washing machine.

"Thanks for washing those stinky things," his wife, Nicole, said as she walked down the stairs to their basement. "You forgot your hoodie though. This thing smells like you haven't ever washed it."

"Yes, I have. Well, I think I have," Josh said with a laugh. "Give it to me."

"How did you get these rips in the sleeve?" she said, holding up the left sleeve before tossing it to him.

"No clue," he said, looking confused. "I must've snagged it on a tree when I was running through the new park. They've got part of the new jogging path finished, so I went through there, but they had part of it blocked off so they can move that house in today. I had to cut through the trees. Disappointing. That hoodie is my favorite."

"Think of it as a battle wound," she said before tossing him the sweatshirt and going back up the stairs.

Chapter 3

"Hey, Red," Officer Evan Willnow said as he stopped to lean in the doorway of Room 27 at the Johnstown Police Department.

It was really more of a large closet that had a desk and four filing cabinets stuffed into it. A single fluorescent fixture was on the ceiling and one of those bulbs was flickering every few seconds. The papers on the desk were stacked neatly and an old Remington typewriter was in the center. The woman at the desk finished typing and then pulled a triplicate form out of the top. She turned with a serious look on her face to stare at the brown haired man in the doorway.

"I think you mean, Detective Elliott," she said, a slight grin breaking through her stern look. "And my hair is not red, it is strawberry blonde."

"Oh, sure," Willnow said, looking down at the cheeseburger in his left hand. "Now that you are a detective you got all fancy on me."

"I'm not fancy," she said, flicking her wavy hair back over her shoulder. "I just know the difference between red and strawberry blonde."

"Ok, whatever. What are you working on?"

"I just finished up the paperwork on those kids that stole some burner phones from Target."

"Well, that certainly sounds like an interesting case."

"Shut up," she said. "You are just jealous of my big office."

"Right, that's what it is," he said with a laugh. "Why aren't you doing it on a computer? You know how to use one, don't you?"

"Chief McMahon has us all doing these reports on a typewriter in triplicate because of the new system. He says he is two years from retirement and has no interest in learning anything new on a computer."

"He does know you can hit print on a computer?"

"I'll let you bring that up to him," she said, putting the form she had just finished into a folder before closing it and tucking it under her arm. "I'm actually on my way to see him right now. I can hardly wait to see how proud he will be of us for recovering those phones."

"Roll those eyes any harder and they'll fall out," he said. "Ah, well, I don't want to steal any of your thunder. I think I'll stop in the breakroom for a cup of coffee and a leftover donut."

"That's disgusting," she said. "The coffee, I mean. It tastes like it was literally set on fire."

"Drink what you brought," Willnow said and turned to walk down the hall, his big laugh filling the length of the corridor.

"Some days I wonder about that man," Elliott said

"Oh, hey, Meredith," Willnow said looking back. "I mean, Detective Elliott, keep me in mind if you need a sidekick on any of these big adventures of yours."

"You wish," she said and took a quick left down the hall that led to the chief's office.

She paused to check her appearance in the ladies' room because the chief was incredibly particular about how his team looked. Meredith Elliott was the first female detective in Johnstown history, and she did not want to leave any room for criticism.

When she walked into the large office at the northwest corner of the building, Chief McMahon was staring at his desk with a tired and angry look on his face. He was listening intently to whoever was on the other end of the phone call. Finally, he glanced up and motioned for her to sit down at his desk.

"Twenty-three years," he said, slamming down his desk phone's receiver.

"I'm sorry, sir?" she said, shifting in her seat and feeling nervous.

"I've been with this department for twenty-three years. I'm two years from retirement and now this happens for the first time. I can't believe it," he ranted before turning to stare out as dusk fell across Milton Park, which occupied one hundred acres just north of the police station.

"What happened?" she asked, placing the burner phone file on the edge of the desk.

"Homicide," he said, without turning around. "This is not something that happens in Johnstown. We don't have murders here."

"When?"

"Dispatch got the call about an hour ago and we had two cars on the scene in less than five minutes. Now, we have looky-loos wandering the neighborhood trying to figure out what's going on. What did you need, Detective?"

"I finished up that case with the stolen phones. You said you wanted to look it over."

"Drop it off in the file room. I don't have time for that now. Besides, those things get stolen daily somewhere around town. It's pointless working the cases at all."

"That could be, sir."

"Was Zinyemba still in his office when you came down?"

"No, I think he went home right at five. His son had a ballgame or something like that."

"Hmm, well, my old man always said the best way to make someone learn to swim was to throw them in the deep end."

"I don't understand."

"You will," he said, turning to look back at her. "I want you to take the lead on this investigation. This is going to be a huge mess and we are going to find out what you're made of. You'll have to do your research and keep things under wraps to make sure there isn't some technicality when we get to trial."

"Yes, sir," she said, leaning back in her chair. A state of shock and excitement flooded through her.

"I'm sure the news people will be all over this before you can get there but try to do some damage control. Who do you want as your backup?"

"I guess I'll take Willnow," she answered.

"That works," Chief McMahon said. "You two were partners, right? That should be just fine for this. Is he still here?"

"Yes, I saw him in the hall on the way to your office."

"Good. Now, get going. I want you to call me with an update as soon as you have anything at all to go on. Let me know if you need anything."

"Yes, sir, and thank you."

"Don't thank me quite yet, Detective Elliott," McMahon said half-heartedly. "Close the door on your way out. I have to call the mayor now. That's always a treat."

Meredith nodded and walked to the door before realizing that the file was still on the chief's desk. She went back to grab it. McMahon sat there waiting for her to leave with his hand on the phone. The case was off to a terrible start.

She dropped the file off on a counter about halfway down the hall, waving to the clerk inside the file room. She could not believe that the chief gave her this assignment but knew she would have to nail it or set back female officers in Johnstown two decades.

"No pressure," she said to herself as she turned to walk toward the break room.

Willnow was watching the nineteen inch TV on an old desk in the corner of the room. He had two bites of his donut left but was caught in a trance. Meredith leaned to her right to see what he was watching.

"...police are on the scene, and we are waiting for a report. Some people in the neighborhood are telling us they know it was a homicide, although we have not confirmed that. The residence belongs to Marsha Benton, however we have no information regarding any victims or suspects. We hope to have an update for you at 9."

"Damn," she said without looking away from the reporter on the screen.

"That's for sure," Willnow said, popping the last bite of donut in his mouth. "I feel bad for whoever gets that case. It's going to be a circus. I bet the chief will give it to Zinyemba, poor guy."

"Nope."

"Nope?" he asked, turning in his chair.

"He gave it to me. Just now."

"Oh, that's no good," he said, taking a drink of coffee.

"And you are my backup," she said, causing him to spray his coffee across the table in front of him.

"That's not funny at all, Elliott!" he said. His eyes were wide as he turned to look at her, hoping she was messing with him. "Tell me you are kidding."

"I'm not kidding," she said. "Now, dry that coffee out of your beard and let's go. Meet me in the lot. I'm taking an unmarked car so we can try to slip in unnoticed."

"Good luck with that," he said, tossing his cup in the trash and grabbing some napkins.

"Five minutes," she said and left the room.

"Yes ma'am," he said, mopping up the mess he had made.

They turned off of Old Johnstown Road at the spot where Marsha had narrowly missed the jogger hours earlier. Elliot's heart sank when she saw the street filled with cars and news vans. All three major stations from San Luis were present and ready to broadcast for the nightly news. Elliott watched the people standing along the street as they crept toward the scene.

Finally, after maneuvering through the small and stubborn crowd, they reached the spot where the yellow tape had been stretched across the road. An officer in uniform was there, instructing people to stay back. The officer visibly relaxed when he saw Willnow get out of the car. It was hard to miss Willnow, since he stood about six and a half feet tall and weighed in over three hundred pounds. Everyone liked him though, because of his sense of humor.

"Hey, Willy," the officer said, lifting up the tape for the big man to duck under.

"Hey, Buckner," he replied, holding the tape up for Elliott.

"Detective," Buckner said, looking surprised, but quickly controlling his expression. "It's the second house on the right. We have two uniforms in back to keep people from sneaking in through the back yard, one at the front door, and two inside. Officer Blackerby was the first on the scene. He can fill you in."

"Thank you, Buckner," Elliott said and continued on toward the house.

Officer Robert Blackerby was standing just outside the front door of Marsha's house. He was writing notes in a small blue notebook and only raised his eyes when Willnow stepped up on the porch.

"Hey, Rob," Willnow said.

"Hey, Willnow," he said. "Hello, Detective."

"Hello, Blackerby," she said. "What have you got for me?"

"Unfortunately, not much. There were no fingerprints on the body, no signs of forced entry, and no clues as to how the killer left the house. The one thing we do have is that Ms. Benton appears to have fought against her attacker. She has one broken fingernail on her left hand and a strand of green fabric wedged under the nail on her right thumb."

"So, we think the killer was wearing a green shirt? That's all we've got?"

"So far, yes."

"Did you get statements from the friends that found her?"

"Yeah, but I think they got here roughly two hours after the murder. It looks like it happened right after she got home. The garage door was closed, and all exterior doors were locked. We haven't found an explanation for how the person got in. Benton lived alone and none of her friends can think of anyone that would have a reason to do this. I've also tried contacting the victim's mother, but no luck so far. She lives in Florida and doesn't have an answering machine."

"Ok, well, it sounds like things are in good order. I'll try calling her mother when I get back to the station."

"That works. I don't like those calls anyway."

"Part of it, I guess," Elliott said. "Are the friends still here?"

"Yes. They are in the family room at the back of the house."

"See if you can get them out of here without letting the media catch on. They don't need any more attention right now."

"You got it."

"Thanks, Blackerby," Elliott said. "Willnow, let's have a look around the garage."

"Yes, ma'am."

Chapter 4

"And let me love you on a back road," Corey Smith sang as his song blasted out of the jukebox at The Quarter Bar. It was a popular dive bar along Westchester Avenue near the eastern edge of Johnstown that drew a wide variety of people.

"Come on big money!" said a woman in a Led Zeppelin shirt from her spot at the video poker machine at one end of the bar. "Mama needs a new pair of shoes!"

"Kris, you know that's not a real slot machine, right?" the man next to her asked.

"Yes, Ken, I can read the sign that says it is for entertainment only and I am entertaining myself. So, keep your comments to yourself, okay?"

Ken snickered, picked up his margarita, and glanced over at two men in suits that looked like they had reached their limit hours earlier. They were watching the end of a Cardinal baseball game, but Ken was sure he recognized them. Maybe they had been there in casual clothes before or maybe he had dealt with them on a work project. People watching was his favorite part of coming to The Quarter Bar.

Gina Walswick, Jill Guess, and Bee Kruzel sat at the other end of the bar, doing their best to ignore the older man trying to talk to them. They had come in after work to unwind and took the only open spot that had room for three but were hoping for one of the tables on the patio.

"So, you all go to school around here?" the man asked.

"No," Gina said. "We are all finished with college."

"Ah, good. Are you all married then?"

"No," she said and then turned back to her friends. She was upset with herself for engaging him at all.

"My name is Ned," he offered. "Can I buy you a drink?"

"No thanks," she said over her shoulder, but made it clear she wasn't turning to talk to him again.

"Can I at least get your name?"

"Tilly."

"Tilly? That's an old lady's name. Is that really your name?"

"Look, I'm just trying to hang out with my friends after a long day at work. If you don't like my name, then pretend it is something else. Either way, just leave us alone."

"Jeez," Ned said. "You don't have to get all upset. I was just talking."

"Ned, you gotta stop bothering women," the bartender said. She had on snug cutoff jean shorts with the pockets sticking out the bottom and a tight, black tank top. She was the most popular bartender at the bar.

"Oh, come on, Jessica! It's a free country and I'm just trying to relax and have some fun. Maybe if you came over and talked to me more often, I would be satisfied."

"Do you need another drink? I've got fifty people in here and I'm busting my butt. I don't have time to chit chat."

"Yeah, I'll have one more. What is this terrible music?"

"Corey Smith. He's one of my favorites, so be nice."

"Well, not everyone can have good taste in music, I suppose."

"Here," Jessica said, putting the frosty bottle on the bar in front of him. "Now, leave them alone or I'll send John down to talk to you."

"John, ha, does he think he's important because this is Johnstown?" Ned said. "You wouldn't do that and he's all talk anyway. Sure, he's six foot five and could bench press a car, but he wouldn't mess with someone that comes here as much as I do. This should be Nedstown."

"Whatever you say, but quit bothering them," Jessica said and walked away, taking an order from two guys who had just sat down.

"Hey, I'm telling you that any of these beautiful young ladies would be lucky to hang out with a guy like me," Ned said to no one in particular. "I've got my red Corvette outside, ready to tear up the roads. It's a convertible and my six disc changer is loaded with music a million times better than this."

The young women were ignoring him, as was Jessica. He looked around, hoping for a reaction, but eventually took a big chug and started watching the people milling around the bar. At sixty-six years old, he continued to pursue the bachelor life he had enjoyed forty years earlier. He refused to acknowledge that time had marched on without him and assumed that he was the prize that all women would fight for. He always visited The Quarter Bar when he knew Jessica was working because he was sure he would win her over eventually. She was five foot nine with long, dark brown hair and he was obsessed.

"Jessica," he called out two minutes later. "Come down here, my love!"

"What do you want, Ned?" she asked. "Did you finish that beer already?"

"No, I just wanted to see your lovely face up close," he said, and she rolled her eyes. "Maybe I'll stick around for closing and you can go for a ride with me."

"You're buzzed and no, Ned. I'm your bartender, not your girlfriend."

"Oh, but the possibilities…"

"Nope, not gonna happen. I need to get back to work."

"Do your thing, I'll watch from over here."

"Great," she said sarcastically and walked away.

Ned watched her make a drink and then turned his attention back to the group of young women. This time he didn't say anything to them, choosing only to nod at them when one would look up at him.

"Let's get out here," Bee said. "That guy is creeping me out."

"Hey, bartender, we need to pay our bill," Jill said, holding out some cash.

Jessica brought them a slip of paper with their total on it on her way to the kitchen.

"Here," Jill said, handing the money to Jessica before she could walk away.

"You need change?"

"Nope."

"Thanks."

"This place isn't bad, except for the old creep."

"Yeah, sorry about that. Maybe move out our patio? I hate to see you all go because of him."

"It was completely full when we got here, and we can't handle him anymore. We'll come back another time, when he's not here."

"I'm sitting right here," Ned said in a playful voice. "You ladies are going to hurt my feelings."

"You have a red Corvette, right?"

"Who, me?" Ned asked. "Why, yes, I do. Did you change your mind?"

"Not at all, but at least we know to avoid coming in when that car is in the parking lot."

"That's just rude," Ned replied, still smiling. "At least one of you will change your mind before you get to your car."

They all shook their heads and rolled their eyes. It was mind-blowing to them that he believed he had a chance with any of them. Jessica frowned as the group of women made their way out the door. Their total spent was double what Ned would spend in a week and their tip for the night was far beyond anything he had ever left. His pathetic pile of change at the end of four or five hours was laughable at best.

"I'm going to go pick out some real music," Ned said and walked toward the jukebox.

"Good. Then, go home and never come back," Jessica said under her breath as she rang in some drinks. She knew she would not be so lucky.

Ned set his drink down on one of the high top tables near the jukebox. The people sitting at the table frowned but didn't say anything. He pulled his wallet from his back pocket and looked around as if someone would be watching him picking out songs. He debated how much to put in the machine and took out a ten dollar bill.

"Ten bucks," he said, looking at the people at the table. "That ought to change the tune around here. Get it?! Change the tune!"

They turned away from him and no one else was paying any attention to him, either. Two couples had come in and taken a booth near the front window. Ned watched them for a minute and concluded that they probably liked country music, too. Ned didn't like country music at all. He would put his ten bucks to good use.

"Ah, I know what will change things up," he said. "My old buddy Nick would be proud of me."

He slipped the ten into the machine and waited for the credits to pop up. He got twelve of them and did a search for one of Nick's favorite artists, Chet Baker. The Quarter Bar patrons were enjoying the sound of The Weeknd, but he knew that would come to an end soon.

"I love this 'play next' option," he said, laughing to himself. "Let's see, now. I'll start with My Funny Valentine, then Almost Blue, and Let's Get Lost. Any others after that and everyone will be falling asleep. Good tunes, but not what these people want to hear. I'll teach them to treat me like that."

The Weeknd finished singing about not being able to feel his face and the slow tune of My Funny Valentine started. He had spent extra credits to jump in line and was pleased when he turned around to see people staring at him in disbelief. Most of them were shaking their heads. But he picked up his beer looking pleased.

"Hey, Jessica, turn it up!"

She ignored him and he was sure he heard her apologize to everyone at the bar. He didn't care what they thought, he was satisfied with the music. He went back to the bar, taking back the spot he had occupied for the last few hours. A man who had been sitting next to him got up and moved away as soon as Ned sat down again.

"Can you skip these songs?" asked a younger guy who took the stool at the end of the bar.

"No, they took that away from us last month," Jessica answered.

"Yeah, no skipping my tunes. I paid good money for these," Ned commented.

"I'd be happy to give you your money back if we could skip them. I came here to have some fun and this crap makes me want to find a bathtub filled with warm water, if you know what I mean."

Jessica smiled and slid a glass of Scotch in front of the man.

"You think you're hot stuff, don't you?" Ned asked.

"I'm just a regular guy who wants to unwind after a long day."

"Well, regular guy, I'm Ned. I spend a lot of money here and I like this music. I think taking half an hour to listen to some good music won't hurt anyone here."

"Well, Ned, my name is Phillip. I spent nine hours today working on plumbing for a new house across town and I'm ready to unwind. I may not spend as much as you, but I'm here for the same reason as all the rest of these fine people."

"That's nice, Phillip," Ned said. "I'm going to have maybe two more beers, figure who wants to take a ride with me in my new Corvette, and then I'm outta here. Until then, I'm going to enjoy my Chet Baker and there is absolutely nothing you can do about it."

"Ned, you need to take it down a notch," Jessica said. "I'll cut you off."

"That's no way to talk to someone who hasn't tipped yet," Ned offered in a sing-song voice.

"Oh, will it be seventy-five cents or maybe even a dollar?" Jessica said mockingly.

"Well, I could take you for a ride in my Corvette after work. That would be worth more than any tip I could leave."

"Right, well, that's never going to happen. Never."

"Never say never," Ned said and turned to look at Phillip, who was twirling a Zippo lighter between the thumb and forefinger of his left hand. "You can't smoke in here."

"Thanks for the update, but do you even see a cigarette?"

"Doesn't matter. You can't smoke!"

Phillip flipped open the lighter and the small flame jumped to life. He held it up pretending to light an invisible cigarette and then took a long drag off of it. Jessica's face lit up just before she walked to the other end of the bar to take a drink order.

"Put it away," Ned said, the playfulness gone from his voice.

"There is no rule against me having a lighter, old man. I can burn up all the butane I want and there is nothing you can do about it. Kinda like me being forced to listen to this music you put on."

"Open flames around alcohol are dangerous, and you're a real idiot for waving that thing around."

"Uh, what? I would bet there isn't more than one or two bottles in this place that would even be remotely flammable. Besides, I'm not drinking that stuff, so you'll have to calm down."

"Put it away! I'm not playing around, asshole."

"What do you have against a harmless little old flame?"

"I'm tired of being nice."

"When did you start being nice? Maybe you should come over here and take it from me."

Phillip clicked the lighter shut and held it at arm's length in Ned's direction. Ned stood up and took a quick step in his direction, but stopped short when Phillip flicked the lighter open again. The blue flame burned true, and Ned's eyes were locked on to it.

"Wait, you're afraid of fire. Aren't you?" he asked.

"Shut up. You're being stupid and careless."

"Nah, I don't think so. I think you are afraid of this tiny little flame," Phillip said, slowly standing up.

"You stay away from me," Ned said, taking a step back. He bumped into a stool and a man who was waiting for his turn to throw darts. "Jessica, do you see what this guy is doing?!"

"I see a guy playing with his lighter," Jessica said. "What do you want me to do?"

"Either you throw him out or I'm leaving!"

"Tough decision there, Ned," she said. "You owe twenty-two dollars, by the way."

"Pay the lady," Phillip said and closed the lighter. Ned stared at him for a moment and then took out his wallet. He took out two tens and a five, tossing the cash on the bar.

"Don't say I never left a tip," he said. "I'll be back when you are in a better mood, Jessica."

"Bye, Ned," she said.

"Bye, Ned," Phillip repeated and lit the lighter again. Ned grimaced and backed all the way to the door.

Once he was outside, he straightened himself up and smoothed out his shirt. He felt the cool breeze chill him as he had started sweating when he saw the flame. No one was standing in front of the bar, so he took a moment to compose himself. He glanced back through the front window and saw Phillip and Jessica laughing together.

"They'll get theirs one of these days."

The Chet Baker song stopped suddenly, and he noticed that Jessica had a remote in her hand. Seconds later, the music of KSHE 95 came rolling out of the speakers. People inside the bar started cheering for the change.

Ned frowned and stomped off toward his Corvette, which he liked to park in a spot far from the building. He didn't want some drunk person banging their door into his baby. Besides, the light over his parking space cast quite a shine on the car, putting him in a much better mood.

One click on his key fob, and the lights flashed on the car. He slid in, running his hands across the tan leather of the steering wheel. The disappointment of the Quarter Bar was a quickly fading memory. Seconds later, the engine roared to life. He gave the accelerator three quick pumps, drawing attention from people sitting out on the patio. While they were watching, he clicked the button to lower the white soft top. Ned looked like a child who just got ice cream as the night sky appeared over his head.

"Come on now," he said softly, looking back toward the patio. He could see that the group of young women he had attempted to flirt with earlier had only moved outside instead of leaving. "I know you all see me and my car. You know I've got money. One of you wants to go for a ride. I know it."

He was not ready to give up on the night, so he turned on his stereo and punched the button to activate the CD player. He waited for a moment and then heard disc four start, which happened to be one of AC/DC's greatest hits albums.

The guitar came on strong and Ned turned the volume way up. Everyone on the patio and probably in the apartment building half a block away could hear Brian Johnson's vocals explode across the night. Highway to Hell was certainly one of Ned's favorites and he liked the Brian Johnson version better than Bon Scott, which had led to many arguments with other fans over the years. Ned began to sing along.

"Living easy, living free. Season ticket on a one-way ride. Asking nothing, leave me be. Taking everything in my stride."

Ned was truly rocking out and was watching the group of young women, especially Gina, as they watched him from the patio. He could see that the two dozen or so people were all looking his way and he loved the attention. He continued singing and pushed the volume higher.

"And I'm going down! All the way! Whoa! I'm on the highway to hell!"

Ned finished off the song with a big swipe of his air guitar. He looked over to the patio. His show wasn't drawing the attention he had wanted, and they had gone back to their own conversations. His show was over, and he hit the power button on the stereo. He considered calling one of his friends, maybe Nick. He wasn't in the mood for smooth jazz anymore.

The silence had become deafening with the lack of AC/DC filling the air. The sound of a shoe scuffing the blacktop on the passenger side of the car drew Ned's attention. He was shocked to see Jessica standing there.

"Well, now, that's a nice surprise. Get in!"

The nearest pole light was casting a shadow on her face, but he could see the outline of the lips that he had loved from the first time he saw it. She grabbed the handle and slid into the seat next to him.

"Is someone else covering the end of your shift?"

She only nodded, looked out through the windshield, and turned the stereo back on, although she turned the volume way down. Ned waited for her to say something but was too excited. His dream was coming true.

"I guess you've had enough talk for one night," he said as a sly smile formed on his face. "Maybe you just want some action."

She turned her head and then shifted her body to face him. Her lips had his full attention, so he did not notice her eyes. He had already put on his seatbelt and forgot this when he tried to turn and it caught, holding him to his seat. Ned laughed nervously for a second and reached for the buckle. Jessica's left hand reached the buckle first, covering it up. She slowly wagged her head from side to side.

"Whatever you want!" he commented out loud.

Jessica tilted her head and brought her right hand to his leg. He could feel the heat coming off of her and he was about to jump out of his skin with excitement. He looked down at her hand, which was starting to slide up his leg. Then, he looked back up at her and saw that she wasn't smiling anymore. He was confused.

The engine revved for a moment, and he looked at the display in the dashboard. Everything looked normal at first, but then he noticed that the engine temperature was climbing. He could feel the hot air coming through the vents and he looked back to Jessica.

This time, he looked into her eyes and realized it was not Jessica at all. He didn't know who it was, but the solid black eyes made him suck in a deep breath. Ned was about to yell when she leaned over and planted a kiss on him that sealed off his call for help. The engine revved again, and flames shot out from under the dash, licking up his legs and onto his chest.

He tried to call out for help again, but she was still kissing him. His eyes were bulging as the pain from the flames raced through his body. Ned grabbed at her hand on the seat belt buckle, trying to free himself. It was useless. Her hand was like a vice, and he felt the fire grow in intensity. The dashboard and leather seats ignited. He tried to free himself, but she kept his head pinned back against the headrest.

No one on the patio noticed what was happening until the entire interior of the car suddenly lit up and made the car look like a dumpster that someone had torched in the middle of the night. Four people jumped up and started running toward the car, although the heat radiating from it was too great for them to get close. They could see two dark shadows in the front seats. The fire department would only find one body.

"Hey!" Gina yelled to Jessica as she ran inside the bar. "There's a car on fire in the parking lot! I think it's the old guy's car."

Jessica was in the middle of pouring a Fat Tire from the tap at the center of the bar and looked up when she heard her yelling.

"Ned's Corvette?" Jessica asked. There was a sharp pain in her left hand, which was holding the tapper, and she jerked it away. A raw, rectangular shape appeared on her hand, as if the tapper had suddenly reached a scorching temperature.

Chapter 5

"Any big plans this weekend, Jorge?" Katherine asked as she stocked supplies in her teller station. They hadn't seen a customer in ten minutes, so making sure they had plenty of deposit and withdrawal slips was a good enough way to pass the time.

"Nope. Nothing except relaxing on my back porch and listening to some music. How about you?"

"I'm going out to Hermann with some of my friends this afternoon. We're going to stay the night at a great little bed and breakfast we found. Should be a good time."

"I bet it will be," he said. "Send me some pictures and I'll pretend I'm there."

"Ok, sure."

"When are you leaving?"

"They are picking me up at my house at 12:30. So, I'm hoping to get out of here right at 12 or at least as soon as the boss lady gets over here to lock the vault with me."

"I'd cover for you if she would let me."

"That's not going to happen, but I'm crossing my fingers that this lull holds out for the next eight minutes. I already have my drawer counted."

"Me, too," Jorge said. "I may not be going anywhere, but I'm getting away from here as soon as possible."

"Oh, hey, did you hear about that fire last night at Quarter Bar?"

"No, did it burn down?"

"The fire wasn't in the bar itself," she said. "Some guy's car caught on fire and burned super fast. He was in it."

"That's awful," he said. "Do they know what caused it?"

"Too soon, I'm sure. It was really late last night and apparently, the guy had just left the bar. A guy I know was there and said they didn't even hear a scream."

"I can't even imagine witnessing something like that."

"Me neither."

"Five more minutes!" called a woman's voice from across the lobby. It was the branch manager, Sarah Wilson. She was pleasant enough, but pretty high strung.

"Crap," Jorge said. "I was hoping to coast to the finish."

"Okay, really quick, you two" Sarah said as she stepped up to the lobby side of the teller windows. "I got an email from corporate today stating that we are way behind on our cross selling. I'm sure you are both trying but pass it along to the others and I'll be putting a memo in everyone's box for Monday. Esad Softic wants us to hand out information with every transaction. He's a firm believer that if we can get two accounts with a customer, they are less likely to bank somewhere else."

"Good old Esad," Jorge said.

"Mr. Softic," Sarah said with a slight smile. "It isn't a big deal. We only need to open fifteen new checking or savings accounts next week plus put in at least eight loan applications."

"That's all?" Katherine said dryly.

"I know, I know," Sarah said, putting up her hands. "He is the regional manager, though, and the suits on high are putting pressure on him."

"Yep, well, I'll get started on that first thing Monday morning," Jorge said. "Right now, I just want to get outside and enjoy this weather."

"I certainly hope you both have a good weekend," Sarah said. "Oh, shoot, I have to call Esad about something really quick. Not more than ten minutes. Katherine, I'll keep it short because I know you want to get out of here."

"Sure," Katherine said, feeling upset that she would have to spend even five extra minutes at work when so much fun waited for her. Sarah walked back to her office and closed the door.

"Sorry about that," Jorge said. "I really would stay."

"Don't worry about it. I'm going to go to the bathroom if you can handle these last couple minutes."

"I can handle it," he said, gesturing to the empty drive-through lanes. "We aren't exactly getting slammed at the moment. I'll make sure to bring in the canisters and lock the doors on my way out."

"Thanks," she said. Her drawer key was on a wristband, and she had it in the lock in one swift motion. It clicked and she hit the key to log off of the teller system. Then, she walked quickly across the lobby and down the short hall that led to the bathrooms. Her phone was already out so she could call Cassie, who was supposed to be picking her up.

The oversized digital clock on the lobby wall changed to 12:00. Jorge immediately tapped each of the red buttons marked 'Return', bringing in the drive-through canisters. They landed on their rubber stoppers, as he powered down each one. A sharp tug on the cord next to the window brought the blinds down. In a matter of minutes, he logged off the system, put his drawer in the vault, grabbed his coffee cup, and locked the lobby doors on his way out. The weekend had arrived.

"Don't tell me," Katherine's friend, Cassie, said as soon as she answered the call.

"Ugh, I know," Katherine said in the privacy of the bathroom after she had locked the door. "Sarah will probably be on the phone for ten minutes or more and I'm stuck here until she is done."

"Can I go pick up your stuff for you or do anything to help out?"

"Not really. Maybe she'll be done sooner, but I might as well talk to you. What's our first stop once we get to Hermann?"

"Oh, you are going to love it," Cassie said.

Thirty feet away, Sarah hung up the phone and ran her fingers through her hair. She turned to look out her window at the Johnstown City Hall, and wished she could get a job there.

Something without weekends would be great. She had exchanged quick waves with Jorge when he left, so she knew the place was locked up.

She left her office and started across the lobby. Sarah noticed Katherine still going through some papers at the drive-through but was not going to work a minute longer than she had to.

"Let's go, Katherine!" Sarah said. "We both have places to be, I think. My car is in the shop, so can you drop me off at the train station? I'm going to take a quick trip to Chicago for a night. Maybe two if I call in sick on Monday."

Sarah stopped at the open vault door and began setting the dials. There were three small clocks that had to be set to the same time or the door would not lock. Also, once the door was locked it could not be opened until the time on the clocks was reached. She glanced over at the rack that held the teller drawers and saw that all of them were in their designated places.

"I see you already put away your drawer, so let's go!" Sarah said.

She heard the door swing between the teller line and the lobby. She was setting the third clock when the footsteps stopped just behind her.

"Took you long enough," Sarah said and looked up. Her fingers brushed past the third dial but didn't move it. Even a single click would have saved her life. Instead, they fell away from the door, and she mouthed silent words as she stared at something like she had only seen in movies.

The clothes matched what Katherine had been wearing and the hair even looked the same, but the skin was pale and damp. The thing in front of her had its mouth hanging slightly open and its eyes were solid black. It was impossible for Sarah to tell if it was looking at her or not. She wanted to yell for help but could not make a sound. There was an alarm inside the vault, but Sarah could not think beyond what was standing six feet away from her.

It stepped forward deliberately and Sarah did not want to wait to find out what happened next. Instinct told her to back up. When she did, the heel of her left shoe caught on the threshold of the vault, and she stumbled backward.

"Don't hurt me!" Sarah yelled as she hit the floor, pulling her arms across her face to deflect an attack. Nothing happened after five long seconds, so she peeked out between her sleeves.

The thing at the door had not moved beyond that first step. Instead, it appeared to be glaring at her because the eyebrows had furrowed slightly. Then, it reached up with its left hand and grabbed the handle of the vault door. With a slight tug, the door started to swing shut. Sarah felt relieved as the giant steel door closed. That passed as soon as she heard the huge bolts in the door snap into place with an empty metal thud.

"Hey!" she yelled. "Let me out of here!"

There was no response and she started panicking. Her heart raced and she was glad she had taken her medicine. She looked up at the vault's ventilation system and took a deep breath.

"Relax, Sarah," she said. "You're going to be fine."

Thinking of that thick steel door protecting her from whatever was out there helped her relax. She settled back against the left wall when she heard the fans slow and then stop. The panic returned. She remembered the emergency phone located behind the panel next to the door. It would ring directly to the police station. She opened the little door and took out the handset.

"Hello?" she said in a shaky voice as she put the phone to her ear. There was nothing other than a thin, cracking sound. "Hello? Someone? Anyone?"

She heard a raspy exhale and knew that the thing in the lobby was on the other end of her call. She slammed the phone back into the box and backed against the wall of safe deposit boxes. Now she was beginning to hyperventilate and tried to calm herself down. It might have worked, but then the lights went out and the fans came back on, only they were pulling the air out of the vault. Without air, she knew she could not survive the weekend.

She felt her chest tighten and her legs went numb. She gasped and tried to scoot toward the door. Finally, she made it to the door and started beating on it.

"Help me! Someone! Help me!" she said in a weak yell.

About that time, Katherine tucked her phone back into her pocket and walked out of the bathroom. The lights in the lobby were off and she stopped to look around, although the room was silent.

"Sarah?" she called. "What are you doing? This isn't funny."

There was still plenty of natural light coming in, so she walked cautiously across the lobby. She gave a wide berth to the teller line in case someone was hiding behind it. Still, there was nothing, but silence and Katherine realized the vault door was closed.

"She did it without me?" she said. "Geez, I was only in there for like five minutes. She must've left."

Katherine looked out the window next to the front door and saw that her car was the only one in the lot. She was growing angry, but let it go so she could just get on her way. The alarm was easy to set with only six quick touches. If she hurried, she could still be ready at 12:30 when her friends would arrive. This made her feel better.

She hopped into her blue VW and started it up. A sudden wave of panic hit her, feeling trapped inside her car. She rolled the windows down a second later and the fresh air relieved her unease. Feeling better, she backed out of the parking space and sped off toward her house.

Chapter 6

Detective Elliott got a precious few hours of sleep that weekend. When she did, it was in her office. She had her wavy hair pulled back into a messy bun and her jacket had been discarded hours ago. The chief had been in to visit her the previous morning, but he promised to give her room to work.

Marsha Benton's mother had flown in the night and driven straight to the Johnstown police department. She had been in hysterics upon arriving, so Elliott had sent her to the Drury Inn two miles away to get some rest. She was still shaken when they picked her up the next morning.

"How did you sleep?" Elliott asked as she placed a cup of black coffee on the table in front of Shelby Benton. It was from QuikTrip. She didn't want to make her drink the stuff from the station.

"Okay, I guess, considering my daughter was murdered and you have no leads on who did it," Shelby replied and took the cup of coffee.

"We are working on it, I promise. We have brought the three friends who found her back in. We are hoping that they will think of a name or anything that could give us some direction."

"I just don't know what to think or do. I told her to come spend some time with me in Florida after her last breakup, but she refused. She would bury herself in work instead."

"I am truly sorry that this is the reason you had to come to Johnstown, but we'll do our best to find out what happened," Elliott said. "Now, can you tell me about this failed relationship? I need to know about anyone who might have a motive in this case."

"Her last boyfriend? His name is Elbert Gunderson," Shelby said. "I can't imagine that he would have done this. The breakup was his decision, I think, and I'm not sure he could have done it, even if he wanted to."

"He couldn't have done it? Why do you say that?"

"Well, he was about two inches shorter than Marsha and not exactly a strong guy. I was told that the murderer choked my baby to death. He wouldn't have been strong enough."

"I think we'll have a chat with him anyway, but it does sound like he is not a likely suspect. Anyone else?"

"Not really. She didn't have much interest in keeping me informed on her personal life, other than who she was dating. I don't think she was seeing anyone as of the last time we talked."

"When was that?"

"Last Wednesday evening. She told me about a get-together with some friends on Friday…"

"We don't have to talk about that."

"Okay," Shelby said, grabbing a napkin to dab at her eyes.

"Did she have any medical issues or medication that you know of?"

"Wasn't she choked to death?"

"She was, but I would like to know anything I can."

"Okay," she said, trying to stop sniffling. "As far as I know, she was still taking her regular medicine for asthma. Other than that, I don't know anything. I wish I had more to offer."

"I'll tell you what, I'll have an officer take you to her house. They can stay with you, just to make sure you don't get any nosy neighbors knocking on the door. I know you have plenty to take care of and maybe something will come to mind. I'm going to talk to her friends again and see if they have anything new."

"Thank you," Shelby said, getting to her feet. "It might be nothing, but something has been bothering me since I found out how she died."

"What's that?" Elliott asked.

"Her biggest fear was not being able to breathe. It came from her asthma or at least that would be my guess. She wouldn't even wear a mask with her Halloween costume as a kid because she found it hard to breathe in one."

"That is definitely something for us to consider when we are investigating. If someone knew that, well, that would be malicious, to say the least."

Detective Elliott walked Shelby out to the front of the police station and arranged for an officer to get her over to Marsha's house. She was frustrated at the lack of leads but knew the chief would be back for an update sometime before lunch. Another cup of coffee and a glazed donut seemed like a good choice as she went back to her office to think. The information was thin, and she hoped something would come to her before the chief arrived.

Thirteen minutes after eleven, Chief McMahon appeared in her doorway. He looked tired, but still tried to look positive.

"How are you doing, Elliott?"

"I'm putting in everything I've got, Chief," she said, turning to look at him.

"I'm sure you are," he said. "What I wanted to know is how are you holding up? This is a big case, and you are doing most of it by yourself. Is Willnow helping you?"

"Sure, Willnow has done everything I ask of him. I'm just not good at delegating. And I guess I'm doing okay, but coffee is definitely not going to hold up for much longer. Sorry."

"What do we have so far?"

"Not much considering how much work has gone into the case. We found no fingerprints or forced entry. There were green threads under the victim's fingernails. The friends had no clue who could have wanted her dead or who would have done it. One friend, Patty, said that Ms. Benton had told her that she had a bad day."

"I'd say that is an understatement."

"Yes, sir," Elliott answered.

"And you have now talked to Ms. Benton's mother?"

"Yes, but she offered only one piece of information. She told me that her daughter was afraid of not being able to breathe. While that is a terrible coincidence, I think it is still a coincidence."

"I suppose so," Chief McMahon said. "I want you to go back and get some rest in the old barracks."

"I'm fine."

"That was an order, Detective Elliott. Get at least six hours of rest and then talk to Zinyemba. He's working on that fire at the Quarter Bar. I think he said there was a coincidence there, too."

"Okay," she replied hesitantly. "I think I'll go home for a bit instead of the barracks, though."

"Fine. Just get some rest. I'll see you this afternoon," McMahon said before turning to walk back along the hallway.

Elliott didn't know what to feel. Part of her craved some rest, but another part made her sure that she would not be able to sleep. She needed to get out of the building for a while, at least. That was what the chief was expecting at the moment. She wasn't sure what to expect from Zinyemba when she got back, but she hoped he wasn't going to be upset that he didn't get the Benton case.

She wanted to go home and sit on the couch. The comfort of home might be what she needed to take the edge off and maybe clear her mind enough to be able to think. She slipped out one of the side doors and got to her car without talking to anyone.

Elliott walked in through the kitchen, tossed her keys and briefcase on the table, and went for the living room. After queueing up one of her favorite playlists, she flopped on the couch. Her brain was racing, but started to slow as the familiar sound of Lisa Loeb's voice filled the room. She began to focus on the lyrics and felt relaxed.

"You say, I only hear what I want to. And you say, I talk so all the time, so…"

Before the song was over, she fell asleep. The dark room and comfortable couch, mixed with extreme fatigue, were exactly what she needed. Luckily, she had set an alarm just before she passed out and woke with a start at 3:30.

"Wow, I gotta get back," she said, jumping up from the couch. She splashed some water on her face and put on a clean shirt. Her hair was still pulled back, but she took a moment to tuck away some strays. "Zinyemba is going to be waiting. Oh well."

Finally getting some sleep made her feel much better. She felt ready to jump back into this case. Tate Zinyemba was at his desk when she walked by, so she stopped in his doorway.

"Hey, Tate," she said.

"Well, now," he said in his baritone voice, turning his desk chair to look at her. His temples were graying, but his mocha-colored skin was unblemished. "If it isn't the woman of the hour."

"Look," she said defensively, "I wasn't trying to start anything with you when I took the case."

"Whoa, whoa, whoa," he said, revealing his pearly white teeth. "What gave you the idea that I wanted the Benton case?"

"Didn't you?"

"No way," he answered. "The first murder in a long time, not much to go on, and the mayor is going to be breathing down McMahon's neck for a solution. That sounds horrible. It's all yours."

"Thanks for painting such a grim picture," Elliott said, smiling.

"Hey, I'd say it was an accurate picture, although I will agree it is grim. Anytime the politicians get involved, I am happy to check out."

"Maybe someday I'll have the option to be more selective."

"Let's hope it is a long time before there is another murder case to worry about. Anyway, what brings you to my humble office."

"I didn't think we'd both fit in my humble office," she said with a laugh. "McMahon told me I should stop by. Something about a coincidence with my case and your car fire."

"Right," he said, looking serious, "the fire seems like an open and shut deal on the surface. The old guy got drunk, started showing off in his fancy car, and something went wrong. The engine caught on fire, probably when he was revving it up."

"So, what's the connection that McMahon was talking about?"

"When I was interviewing people that had been at the scene, I talked to a Phillip Sneed. He was pretty shook up and it didn't make much sense to me. He was inside when the fire happened and was not even one of the people who made it outside in the first few minutes."

"And?"

"Patience, my young padawan. Both Phillip and Jessica, the bartender on duty, said the victim had left the bar only minutes earlier. He had apparently freaked out over a lighter, tripping over himself on his way out the door. Jessica said she had never seen anyone that afraid of a flame and then for him to die like that was a horrible coincidence."

"That is certainly disturbing," Elliott said, thinking about her conversation with Shelby Benton. "If he really was afraid of fire, then that could be the connection McMahon was talking about. My victim's mother said that her daughter was deathly afraid of not being able to breathe."

"But, mine is an accident and yours is a murder."

"Maybe?" Elliott said with a shrug of her shoulders. "I mean, it *is* a strange coincidence."

"Sure, but both deaths happened within hours of each other. We have nothing else connecting those two people and who would have known the greatest fears of both of them?"

"I've got nothing," Elliott said, slumping against the doorframe. "It sounds like there is more to this story, but what?"

"I'll tell you what," Zinyemba said. "Let's both take a bit and look through each other's notes. Look for anything, I mean anything at all, that sounds like a connection."

"That works for me. We can team up on this."

"Oh no you don't," he said, wagging his finger at her. "You are still the lead on the Benton case, and I'll keep to my lowly car fire."

"Gee, thanks."

"Here are my notes," he said, taking a folder from his desk. "I'll walk down to your office and get your notes. You can give me a call when you are done."

Elliott agreed and they went to retrieve the Benton notes. The next hour went by quickly as she studied the statements given by the dozen or so people who had stuck around to talk to the detective on the night of the fire.

Reading the statements of buzzed or drunk people was painful, although she was glad that she hadn't been the one to talk to them. She had done that sort of thing enough times as a beat cop.

The consensus was that the deceased was being a jerk of the highest order and trying to show off for a group of young women who had apparently turned away his advances. Two patrons talked about hearing him crank up his stereo in the minutes before the fire and others talked about him revving the engine on his Corvette, which had drawn some attention for a moment.

The statement given by Phillip Sneed was certainly sobering and had shaken him to the core. He had been one of only two people who were completely clear on what had happened. He felt horrible about the lighter but swore he had been playing around. He told Zinyemba that he hoped they didn't think he started the fire.

The bartender, Jessica, had a strange blister on her hand, which was interesting. However, there was no way she was in the car since the security footage showed her inside the bar the entire time. Elliott was deep in thought about the situation when her desk phone rang, causing her to jump.

"Hello," she said after grabbing the handset.

"Elliott," McMahon said, "I want you in my office as soon as you can get here. We have another connection that is going to cause quite a stir. The mayor will be here in an hour. I want to stay ahead of this thing."

"On my way," she said. The phone had barely landed in its cradle before she grabbed Zinyemba's file and trotted off toward the chief's office. She had a sickening feeling about what was about to happen.

Elliott paused when she entered the chief's office. McMahon, Zinyemba, and another man she did not recognize were already there. She could tell that he was from the San Luis County Police Department, based on his uniform.

"Have a seat, Elliott," McMahon said, gesturing toward the only empty chair in front of his desk. "This is Detective Jason Bower. He's with the County Police and, well, I think I'll let him share what he has."

"Thank you, Chief," Bower said, turning to look at Zinyemba and Elliott. "This morning, we got a call from Southern National Bank. Apparently, their regional security system supervisor had their emergency call button set to ring through to us instead of your department. The man on the phone, a Jorge de la Cruz Delgado, was beyond hysterical.

We responded instead of relaying the call. When our officer arrived, there were about a dozen people standing at the entrance to the bank, trying to figure out why they couldn't get in. The officer tapped on the door and got the attention of one of the employees, who promptly let him in, but locked the door behind them. The man who had made the call was pacing across the lobby, looking panicked. The woman who let him in was visibly shaking but was able to talk to him. She said that when they arrived at the bank, they were surprised that their branch manager was not there, and they were not able to reach her on the phone.

They went ahead and unlocked the vault, so the bank could open on time. That's when they found the manager's body curled up in the fetal position at the center of the vault. Neither could guess how she got in there since the procedure required two people to lock up at the end of the day."

"So, she suffocated?" Zinyemba asked. "That's awful."

"It looks like that's what would have happened," Bower said.

"But?"

"They said she went into cardiac arrest, probably from anxiety. We found medication in her desk. They took the body back to the lab to do an autopsy, but they didn't have anything further for me."

"Three unusual deaths in Johnstown in a matter of days is going to draw attention to the city that Mayor Westchester does not want," McMahon said. "He will want answers and he will want them yesterday."

"We can't give him what we don't have," Zinyemba said.

"The thing is," McMahon said, "when I was looking over the statements that Detective Bower so graciously supplied, I saw that one of the tellers commented that the deceased had often refused to go in the vault because she was claustrophobic. Now, that might be a coincidence again, but I am beginning to doubt it. All three deaths were by a method that directly tied to their fears."

"If that's the case, then we have some sort of serial killer on our hands," Bower said with a frown.

"A good one," Elliott said. "There have been no fingerprints, no trace evidence, and no video footage."

"Not even at the bank?" Zinyemba asked.

"If they had the killer on video, then they would be out looking for them right now," Elliott replied.

"Well done, Detective," Bower said, giving a slight nod of approval before frowning again.

"So, what do we do next?" Zinyemba asked. "There is obviously a connection here. If there is a serial killer, what is the common thread? We know the attacker is using their fears, but that would definitely take a lot of planning and time. I would think they would have to know the person pretty well. Who knows all of these people?"

"We tell the mayor what we have and that it really needs to stay low-key. The media is on it, but we need to keep people from freaking out," Elliott said.

"Detective Bower," McMahon said, "it looks like this is going to be a big case and has the potential to get much bigger. Would you be interested in working together so we can try to contain this?"

"I think that would be a good plan," Bower said, placing three of his business cards on the desk. "Please let me know if you come up with anything and I'll have the coroner update you as soon as the autopsy is complete. Now, I'm going to get back out there. I have a bad feeling that this isn't over."

"Thank you and we will be talking to you soon," McMahon said as he stood to walk Bower to the door. They went out into the hallway, leaving Elliott and Zinyemba alone.

"This is way more than I imagined it would be," Elliott said.

"Look, we are in this together," Zinyemba said. "You are still on lead and need to make it known that you are in control. Willnow will make sure the officers follow your lead and I'll keep the other detectives busy. Where are you going to start?"

"I guess I'll start looking for something or someone that each of the victims had in common. Their method of death isn't enough. I think there has to be something else."

"I agree," Zinyemba said. "It seems the murderer is punishing them in the worst ways possible."

"Complex is the best word I can think of," Elliott said. "I'm guessing we don't have much time until we have another victim, so let's get to it."

Chapter 7

"Good work today, boys!" said Pat Ryan, crew chief for West County Surveying. "Two days in and we're ahead of schedule. One more ten-hour shift and we can turn this over to the computer nerds. Hopefully they'll be good to go with what we have."

"You buying the first round?" asked Sean Foote, as he leaned against one of the trucks.

"We will knock this out tomorrow and I'll buy two rounds!"

The team of five cheered for this announcement and started packing up.

"Sean, you are in charge of measuring that well first thing in the morning."

"Aye, aye, cap'n!"

"You're so strange."

"Probably because it's hot out here."

"You're always strange, Foote," said one of the other guys.

"There we have it," Pat said and glanced over at a truck pulling up at the site. "Oh, good, the construction guys are back. You boys finish up and get out of here. I'll see you in the morning."

"How's it coming?" Bill Kelly asked, as he and Tony came across the lot.

"I think we'll have everything wrapped up by tomorrow. These ALTA surveys are a pain in my ass. However, I think we can be ready to set elevation markers by tomorrow afternoon."

"Sounds great. The mayor is checking in about eight times a day to see where we are. He wants the land movers in here, but I'm doing my best to keep him happy with any progress we can show."

"I'm glad I don't have your job, then!"

"I wonder why I do it sometimes," Bill said. "Have you checked that well, yet?"

"Just got the location of it. I'll have my crew measure the depth tomorrow. Shouldn't affect the survey too much."

"Works for me. Are you done for tonight?"

"Yep, we'll be back at seven."

"Alright, well, have a good one."

"You, too, Bill," Pat said and went straight to his truck. He didn't want to take a chance on needing to answer any more questions.

Once he turned out onto the road, Bill said, "Looks like they covered the well with plywood, but hopefully they won't mind if we take it off. I want to have the first look down there. Those guys aren't really working for us, so anything they find would go straight to the mayor."

"Are you expecting to find anything?"

"No, but let's not have the mayor coming to take a look."

"Good plan," Tony said and strode over to the well, avoiding some ruts. Bill was close behind. They took hold of opposite sides of the sheet of plywood and walked it away. "We've got about two hours of sunlight left."

"Somehow, I don't think sunlight is going to help us much. It's going to be dark down there no matter what," Bill said. "We will just have to use headlamps."

"Okay," Tony said. "Also, I'm going to throw it out there that this whole thing creeps me out. My throat tightens up when I think about that fog or whatever that came out from under the house."

"I'm with you, but I'm more afraid of Jack Westchester causing trouble for us. He's already called Mr. Freemantle twice. I feel like a third time would not be good on my first time out as project lead."

"Fair enough. I guess we better get busy. Maybe there is nothing down there and this will be over in a matter of minutes."

"I hope so," Bill said. They went back to the truck, and he opened one of the side doors on the utility bed. He took out a work belt and headlamp. Tony did the same and nodded when he was ready.

They didn't talk as they walked over the now vacant lot where the Westchester home had stood. The orange flagging flapped gently in the breeze, but it felt like a gale force wind to Bill and Tony. They pulled all the lath from the ground and tossed them to the side. Getting to their knees, they stared down into the darkness.

They both held their breath, afraid that the smell they had encountered before would be there again. This time, there was nothing and they exhaled simultaneously. Tony picked up a small stone and dropped it into the well. Not quite two seconds later, there was a brief splash that echoed up the well.

"Not gonna lie," Bill said. "I was hoping it would be dry. Grab a roll of string and a weight. We are going to check the depth ourselves really quick. I want to know how far down it is to the water at least."

Tony nodded and walked back to the truck, where he got a one hundred foot roll of line normally used for making level lines and a pair of rusty pliers he had found at a previous job. He tied the line on tight and went back to the well.

"I think this will work," he said. "The pliers should be heavy enough to find the depth of the water, too."

"Great," Bill said, pulling a marker and a tape measure from his belt. "Let's mark it in three-foot increments."

Dozens of cars went by on Westchester Road, but few of the people in them even noticed the two men on their hands and knees where the old house had been. The ones who saw them didn't care.

Minutes later, they heard a bloop as the pliers broke the surface of the water. Bill grabbed his tape measure to check how far past the last mark they were. A quick computation told him it was a lot deeper than he had guessed.

"Seventeen feet, three inches," he said.

"I can barely see the ripples on the water," Tony replied, looking down into the well.

"Is it just water or can you see something else?"

"Just water, but it looks like tree roots have worked their way through the bricks about ten feet down."

"That's fine," Bill said. "I'm not worried about the roots."

"Should we check the depth of the whole well?"

"Might as well. Let me know when you feel it go slack."

The line slipped further into the well. Bill frowned as he had hoped it would only be less than six inches of water. Finally, the pliers came to rest on the bottom.

"Let's see," Bill said, pulling out his tape again. "The water is four and a half feet deep. That's no good."

"It didn't feel like there was anything else down there," Tony said. "I'm sure we're fine."

"I hope so, but it is a lot easier to hide something in four feet of water instead of four inches."

Tony started pulling the line back up and felt it catch after only eight inches. Bill saw the progress stop and looked down into the well. Their combined light allowed them to see the top of the water clearly, but there was only the slightest disturbance from when the pliers had stopped.

"Give it a pull and see if it comes loose," Bill said. Tony did just that and the pliers moved about two inches before pulling back down.

"I think it is caught on something that has some give to it, probably another root."

"Give another good pull. I really need that to be a root."

"Maybe it's a treasure chest," Tony said.

"I'll take that bet," Bill said, still looking down in the well.

Tony started to pull again and applied more pressure, but he did not want to break the line. A half second before he was going to give up, the resistance stopped, and the line lurched up. The stress on the line was relieved, but Tony was not.

"What is it?" Bill asked, studying the surface of the water.

"I don't know, but it felt like something broke loose. I have a really bad feeling about this. I think I hooked something. It's pretty heavy. Maybe we should just cut the line and say there is nothing down there. We can get equipment in here and fill it with dirt."

"No, we can't do that. The survey crew will be back tomorrow, and the mayor gave specific instructions to make sure this well isn't a problem."

Tony nodded with a frown and started pulling the line in. His hands were shaking with each slight pull. He could tell there was significantly more weight on the line than when he had dropped it into the well. The feeling of wanting to be sick was getting the best of him as he watched one of the measurement lines move toward him. The pliers would be out of the water soon, along with whatever he had caught.

"There," Bill said, pointing into the well.

The handle of the pliers that the line was tied to came out of the water and Tony paused. He was not sure he wanted to know what was on the other side. Bill made an executive decision and took hold of the line. He gave a slow pull. The pliers emerged from the water with their discovery and both men studied it, trying to see what they had found.

"Definitely not a root," Bill said, shaking his head.

"No. I think it looks like… like a…"

"Yeah. It looks like a skull."

Bill was still holding the line when Tony let it go. He ran from the well and doubled over before he got to Ballpark Drive. He heaved up his dinner and then collapsed backward onto the torn-up grass. Tony was gasping for breath as he wiped his mouth on his sleeve. Bill had watched him run away but didn't move. Instead, he started pulling the skull up. He was hoping that it was an illusion and that there could not possibly be a skeleton at the bottom of the well.

Five minutes later, Bill dialed the mayor's cell number while staring at the perfectly intact skull on the grass three feet in front of him. It was a horrendous sight, and it was far beyond Freemantle's contract with Westchester.

"Bill? How are you doing this fine Monday evening?"

"I've been better, but I think you need to come to the building site."

"The survey crew should be done. Is something wrong?"

"Definitely," Bill said flatly. "The well we found under the house wasn't empty."

"What is it, Bill?" Jack said, the sound of concern and fear heavy in his voice.

"I… think you should come have a look for yourself."

"I'll be there in four minutes," the mayor said.

Chapter 8

Tuesday morning brought a light rain under an overcast sky. It was gloomy, but strangely calm. However, two sisters, Deb and Sarah Dhue, were not deterred from their morning walk. They had joined the Silver Striders walking club at Westchester Commons when Deb turned sixty-two.

The indoor track at the rec center was about an eighth of a mile long, but both Dhue sisters preferred it to using a treadmill. It gave them a chance to talk about life and watch people, which helped them both develop characters for their writing. Deb liked writing poetry and short stories, while Sarah had been writing novels for many years.

The best part about getting to the Commons before eight in the morning was avoiding the meat heads, as they called them. The grunting and yelling were awful. The only drawback to the track was that it ran right between two sections of free weights, so it was like a tunnel of noise if they came in too late.

"So, how's your new book coming along?" Deb asked as they walked along the section of track suspended over the basketball courts. This was her favorite part of the track because she had always been a fan of basketball and there were six large windows looking out on the small park in front of the building.

"I'm in a bit of a lull. I need to come up with a minor problem for the main characters to overcome. Gotta fill some pages," Sarah said.

"Main characters? That is probably your first problem. Call them by name. Everyone knows that getting in their head is the best way to write."

"Right, well, then I need something for Jan and Don Stover to figure out. They are sleuthing outside of Greenville, Illinois in this book."

"How many Jan and Don novels have you written? Seventeen?"

"Sixteen. This will be number seventeen. Not sure how many more I have in me."

"Ah, the possibilities are endless. I still don't know how you manage to put so many words together. My ten thousand word short stories are the best I can do."

"And you have a special talent for telling a great story in so few words," Sarah said. "I just wish you'd stop killing my favorite characters."

"Thanks, but I'm thinking about trying something new," Deb replied. "And you know I can't stop killing your favorites. Your reaction makes me smile every time."

"One of these days I'm going to write a book about an author, and I'll kill her," Sarah said. "It's you."

They both laughed at that, but soon heard heavy footfalls on the track behind them, so they instinctively moved to the inside lane. Sarah glanced back over her shoulder to see a young man with arms bigger than her body trotting toward them. He had earbuds in and grinned when he saw her looking.

"Morning, ladies," he said on his way by. The thin material of his running shorts swished, and they frowned at the poor excuse for a shirt that he was wearing. To them, it was more like the remains of a shirt.

"Gross," Deb said after he had disappeared around the big curve ahead.

"Maybe he's one of those guys that runs two fast laps trying to look cool and then calls it a day," Sarah said. "No stamina, just a showoff."

"Hopefully so. He seems like a guy with little stamina," Deb said, and they giggled.

They continued on around the curve into a sort of tunnel that ran between a workout room and the outside wall of the building. In about thirty seconds, they would emerge into the free weight area, and they hoped the guy would not be there. They both gave a sigh of relief when they saw that he wasn't there or at the water fountains to their left.

"Great, he's gone," Sarah said. "Now, how many poems have you written since we walked last week?"

"Two, but they are still works in progress. I like the premises, but the wording isn't quite right."

"And what are they about?"

"The first one is about the blistering heat we've been dealing with and the second is about being kind to those around us," Deb said. "Kinda hard to work on them at the same time since the heat basically makes me want to break things."

"I'll walk further over this way, I think."

"Very funny."

They reached the part of the track that was elevated over the basketball courts again, but there was still no sign of the meathead. Four more Silver Striders had joined them on the track. Three others split off to use a stair climber or treadmill.

As they approached the end of the tunnel on their next lap, they heard the slam of weights and knew the guy was not gone. It was their normal practice to ignore anyone working out, so they kept talking about their writing.

"Huuuuu yaaaahhhhhh," the guy yelled as they walked past. "Hup hup hup hup hup!"

His voice carried throughout the building and Deb could not stop herself from rolling her eyes.

"That's simply ridiculous and totally unnecessary," she said.

"Gooooooo Keegan goooo!" the guy's voice called from behind them.

"He's probably compensating for something," Sarah offered.

"Oh, I'm certain," Deb said. "And his name is Keegan?"

"I guess so. What ever happened to names like John or Tom or even Colby?" Sarah asked. Deb smiled at the last name.

It only took about two minutes to make a lap. They went past him a half dozen times, shaking their heads when he would yell out some nonsense word every time he lifted. Both of them refused to even look at him.

"What do we have, three more laps?" Sarah asked.

"Yeah, that'll put us right at four miles," Deb replied. "I don't hear the grunting and yelling. Maybe he left?"

"We should only be so lucky."

They went through the tunnel again. On the other side, they saw the guy leaning against a support beam and staring at them.

"Well, hello ladies," he said and whistled a cat call in their direction. "I didn't know the hotties came to the gym this early."

"You are disgusting," Deb said, but the guy only laughed. He mopped off his forehead with a thick white towel and turned back to the weights.

"Let's cut it short and finish up on the treadmill," Sarah suggested.

"Good," Deb said, and they took a sharp left to get to the machines.

"I hope he doesn't fall and hit his head. He might hurt his tiny little brain," Sarah said after getting a quick drink of water. "Or any other tiny thing."

"You're vicious today."

Half an hour later, the meat head walked past them on his way to the spiral stairs that led down to the lobby and locker rooms. He gave them each a wink. They would only see him one more time.

The older man at the front desk was training two of the younger workers on the membership system when he went by. He gave a laugh in their direction and shook his head. Working the desk at a place like this was far below anything he would ever do.

He turned right along a short hallway and glanced through the glass on his left to see people shooting hoops. He did not like games and especially did not like watching people play stupid sports like basketball. The door to the locker room was on his right and he went in.

Two coves of smaller lockers were in the first section of the room. He always considered this to be the area for beginners and moved on toward the back section, where full-sized lockers were available to hold all his gear. One older man was sitting on a bench in the second cove of small lockers. He was drying his hair and looked up as Keegan walked by.

"Boo!" Keegan yelled at him, stomping one foot in the old man's direction. The man jumped. He started laughing again as he continued on his way.

The area with the larger lockers was empty, as usual for the mornings. Keegan was not the modest type, so he stripped down right in the middle of the locker room. He did not care who might walk through and was proud of how he looked. After looking himself over in the mirror and even kissing his biceps, he grabbed his towel and shower kit.

"Looking good, big boy."

The showers were in the rear section of the locker room, and he took the third shower stall. He hung his towel on the hook outside and stepped in to turn on the water. He preferred near scalding showers, so he had to wait for the temperature to climb. Finally, the steam started rolling out over the shower walls and he stepped back in.

"Now, that's what I'm talking about," he said as the hot water washed over him. "Good workout, Keegan. We'll do better tomorrow. Benching four hundred isn't good enough anymore."

He started to hum as he squeezed a blob of Axe body wash into his left hand. The suds formed quickly, and he inhaled the pungent scent, which he equated with manliness. He was sure the women would be flocking to him any moment, as promised by the ads.

Minutes later, shampoo from the matching bottle filled his hand. He lathered it up before scrubbing his recently tightened buzz cut. He used too much but did not care because he wanted to be fully covered in the masculine scent.

The lights flickered and he paused for a moment, then they came back on.

"Stupid kids. They should be at school or something," he said.

The lights went out again and the room was completely dark. He waited for about thirty seconds and then started rinsing his hair. The suds swirled around the drain as he twisted the knob to turn off the shower.

"Turn the lights back on you little idiots!" he yelled from the shower area after flinging open the curtain.

The lights came back on, and he nodded, knowing he had scared them. He grabbed his towel to start drying off when the lights went out again. This time the emergency lights came on, which was odd.

The fluorescents lit up again and he waited. He heard some light footsteps and then the lights went out again. This time, only a single emergency sign stayed on. It was in the area where his locker was, so he wrapped the towel around his waist and started in that direction.

"Look, whoever is messing with the lights better stop! If that's you, old man, I'm going to mess you up."

Silence was the response. He heard more footsteps. They sounded like they were coming from the front section. He knew it had to be the old man he had seen on his way in.

"I'm serious! You are *truly* going to regret this!"

He walked around the corner into the area where his locker waited. The single bulb glowing on the exit sign near his locker drew his attention. He looked around to see if anyone was there, but he saw no one.

"Fine," he said and walked toward this locker. He was about fifteen feet away when that single bulb went out. "Hey!"

The footsteps suddenly sounded heavier and seemed to be coming from the direction of the smaller lockers. He squinted his eyes, trying to see anything, although the room was completely dark. He took a fighter's stance and prepared himself. The footsteps stopped and he could feel the silence closing around him.

"I'm not afraid of you!"

"I know you aren't," a calm woman's voice replied. Keegan turned toward the voice, ready to fight. "I know what you are afraid of though."

"Are you one of the women from upstairs? This isn't funny."

"Funny? It was never meant to be funny," the woman replied, only this time she was behind him. He spun around to face her. She was still invisible through the wall of darkness.

"You don't know anything about me!"

"Oh, yes, I certainly do," she said, now back in the spot where she had started. He turned back in that direction. "You are afraid of the dark."

"That's ridiculous. Now, turn the lights on!"

"I can smell your panic and fear in the air."

"Ok, weirdo," Keegan said. "I'm done with this. Show yourself!"

"I don't think you really want that."

"Yes, I do! Are you afraid that I'm going to beat you down?"

"As you wish."

The emergency lights clicked back on, and he saw the woman at the edge of a shadow. He realized it was one of the women he had been teasing. He laughed.

"The joke's over," he said.

"Indeed," she said and took a step into the light. Keegan saw that the outfit was right, but the eyes were all black. Her face was oddly blank, and he took a step back. She took a step forward.

"What are you doing?" he said, letting his arms fall. "I'm not afraid of you!"

"Not me, but you are afraid of the dark," she said, and the lights went out again.

He took two more steps back but did not hear her move. He had been in that locker room hundreds of times and knew how to get to his locker. The bank of full-size lockers was where he needed to get, so he turned to move that way as quickly as he could. As he rounded the corner, his damp feet slipped on the concrete floor. He balanced himself against the wall and kept going. One more step and then he would turn into the cove with his locker.

The lights flashed on as he started to make the turn, blinding him for an instant. She was standing between him and his locker. He threw up his hands in a defensive motion, trying to stop his momentum. His feet slipped again, only this time he had nothing to balance himself with. He spun mid-air as his feet went out from under him and the lights went out again just as the side of his head struck the corner of the wooden bench that stood in the center of the cove. The impact snapped his neck.

Thirty minutes later, the Dhue sisters started down the stairs from the exercise area.

"Do you have time to get a cup of coffee over at Maeva's?" Deb asked.

"Sure," Sarah said, but then glanced down at the lobby. "What's going on?"

They both stopped on the open staircase and watched as a police officer was talking on his radio, while two paramedics rolled a stretcher toward the locker room.

"Something serious it looks like," Deb said. "Why would the police be here?"

"I don't know," Sarah said and motioned for them to continue down the stairs. They arrived in the area outside the locker room entrances and looked around.

"I'm sorry, ladies," the police officer said. "I'm going to have to ask you to move on into the locker room or wherever you were going."

"What happened?" Sarah asked.

"There was an accident in the men's locker room."

The sisters started toward their changing area when the men's door opened, and the stretcher came out. A sheet was over the body, but they both saw the bulging arms and knew exactly who it was. They knew he was dead, and a cold chill ran over each of them, thinking back to the angry thoughts they'd had about him a short while earlier.

Chapter 9

"Jim!" Elizabeth Donald screamed from the kitchen, rousing her husband from his sleep. "Get in here!"

Jim sat up and rubbed his eyes. He had fallen asleep watching the 1954 version of Godzilla. It was black and white and low tech compared to the new ones, but it was still his favorite. A great scene was about to begin but did not delay in getting to the kitchen.

He was pretty sure he knew why she was yelling, and he was growing tired of it. His slippers shuffled along the hall, and he heard four distinct slaps from the flyswatter that had become something of an appendage for his wife.

"I can't do this anymore!" she yelled at him as soon as he turned the corner into the kitchen.

"I've tried everything except an exterminator and those guys charge an arm and a leg," Jim said. "Maybe it will get better when the weather cools off."

"An arm and a leg? Well, how much does a hotel cost? I'll be staying there until these spiders are gone. No more. You know I hate these things."

Three small spiders raced across the backsplash behind the stove and Jim could only stare. He knew that if he killed those three, there would be five more to take their place. Dozens of trips to Menards, Lowe's, and Home Depot resulted only in a pile of ineffective insect repellent bottles.

"But it's your dream house, my love!"

"Yeah, well, it's turning into my nightmare house. There was one on your toothbrush this morning and two came up out of the drain while I was in the shower."

"Did you get rid of the one on my toothbrush?"

"I smashed that thing, but it smeared right across the bristles."

Jim wrinkled his nose at the image of spider guts where his toothpaste should go. The only option was to dump what little cash they had left into this problem.

"Fine, I'll call an exterminator. I guess this problem is bigger than what I can handle."

"Good," she answered. "I was up until after midnight researching local exterminators. Here is the one with the best reviews online."

Jim looked at the paper she handed him, then up to her eyes, and back to the paper.

"Creepy Crawly Extermination Company?"

"Yes."

"Are you sure it wasn't one of the Onion articles you like?" he asked with a laugh as he looked back up. He saw she was in no mood to joke about this, so he nodded. "Alright, I'll try to get them out here today."

"I'll be packing a bag."

Jim picked up his phone from the small table in the hall they used to hold keys and such things. He looked back to the paper in his hand and shook his head, not wanting to admit defeat. He heard the suitcase bang against the doorframe of the bedroom closet, and he dialed the number.

"Hello! Creepy Crawly Extermination! We will kill the creepy crawly critters that drive you crazy."

"Right," Jim said, wanting to hang up after that overzealous introduction. "Okay, I need some help with spiders."

"Ah, yes, spiders can be a challenge. How soon do you need me to come out?"

"Last week would be acceptable."

"Shoot! Can't help you there, pal, but I will be finished up on my current job in about an hour. Tell me about your situation."

"Spiders. They are everywhere. It doesn't even seem to be one kind, although I don't think we have any of those brown recluse things."

"That's good. Do you know where they are coming from and what have you tried?"

"I've tried everything I can get from the local home improvement places. I was hesitant to buy anything off the internet because of not knowing exactly what I was getting into. Some of those online places are sketchy."

"Probably a good plan and they are usually overpriced."

"Speaking of price," Jim said. "How much do you think this is going to be?"

"I don't know much about the job yet, but I think I can stay under five hundred. It will depend on how much time I have to spend crawling into tight places and how much of the house is infested."

"That's not too bad, I guess."

"I doubt you'll beat that price for what you have told me so far."

"Okay, we will see soon," Jim said. "What's your name?"

"I'm Scott McKing and I'll be there in less than an hour. I'm probably going to fog your house, so you'll need to stay somewhere else for two or three nights."

"My wife has already packed and I'm hoping that no spiders got in the suitcase."

Forty-seven minutes later, a small green van with neon yellow lettering stopped in front of the Donald house. CCEC was written on the side of the van and a picture of a cartoon man spraying a bug adorned the passenger door.

An energetic-looking man with long red hair and wearing a green jumpsuit came bouncing out of the van. He went to the back and opened the double doors to retrieve some equipment. A narrow smile showed between his mustache and beard. He loved his job.

Scott took out a silver cylinder that he slipped on like a backpack and then pulled a dark leather work belt around his waist. The wand from the cylinder clipped onto the right side of his belt, making him look like he was ready to do battle with some bugs.

As he walked up the sidewalk to the Donald house, he glanced to his right and saw a boy of about five peering at him through the picket fence around the neighboring house.

"Hello, little man!"

"Hi."

"I'm Scott. I'm an exterminator. That means I kill bugs and pests."

"My little sister is a pest."

"Well, I can't help with little sisters," he said with a laugh. "Spiders, roaches, and mice are more my specialty."

"Oh."

"I'm going to be spraying some things to help get rid of some spiders at your neighbor's house. It is really bad for people to breathe, especially children. Can you promise to stay in your yard today?"

"I can't go outside the fence without my mom or dad."

"That sounds good," Scott said. "If you see a spider run out, just step on it."

"Okay!" the boy said.

He gave the boy a wave and went up the steps, striding directly to the front door. He thought it was appropriate for a house overrun by spiders to have a brown front door. He gave three quick knocks and stepped back to wait. The door swung open a moment later and Jim smiled, the relief evident on his face.

"Wow! You got here fast. Thank you."

"I told you less than an hour and I always aim to please," Scott said, and Jim motioned for him to come inside.

Elizabeth marched out of the hallway leading to their bedroom with a frown on her face and a suitcase in her left hand. She glanced at the exterminator, who was grinning, but she continued on her way out the door.

"Sorry," Jim said, "she is really upset with this whole situation. I probably waited too long to bring in a professional."

"Better late than never!"

"I'm not sure she would agree with that, but I'll hope for the best once these spiders are gone."

"Let's have a look at the problem, shall we?"

"Right this way," Jim said and started toward the kitchen. He showed Scott the spiders crawling along the tops of the cabinets, behind the fridge, and under the table. Then, they went to the master bedroom to see spiders scurry across the throw pillows and a dozen or so crawling across the sink. He noticed the spider mashed on Jim's toothbrush.

"I'm not sure a toothbrush is the best tool for killing spiders," he commented.

"Tell me about it, but that was a not so subtle message from my wife."

"What have you used so far?"

"We can go down to the basement and look at all the empty spray bottles. I've also used five different foggers from Lowe's, but nothing seems to work for more than three or four hours."

"Are there spiders down there?"

"Oh yeah. Too many to count really. The oldest part of the house is on a crawl space that has a dirt floor and is hard to get around in. They seem to be coming from there, but I haven't found a nest or anything to focus on."

"Then, that is where I come in," Scott replied. "I have some stuff that you can't pick up at Lowe's or Home Depot, if you know what I mean."

"Yeah, I'm depending on you having the good stuff. Otherwise, Elizabeth is going to want to burn this place down."

"I don't think it will come to that."

Jim turned the knob on the narrow door that led to the basement. The stairs were squeaky and quite steep. A small note card was taped on the floor joist above the bottom of the stairs, telling people to 'Duck or Bump'. Scott found this amusing and elected to duck.

They went to the right and then under the stairs to a small square door. Scott could see some tiny spiders slipping out between the wooden door and the concrete wall. He also took note of all the empty bottles stacked along the wall. It looked like Jim had, in fact, tried everything available to remedy this problem. He knew that there was certainly a problem, but it could be handled with some of his commercial-grade spray.

"I think I can have this under control within an hour or two," he commented.

"You better look in the crawl space before making that claim," Jim said as he walked over and lifted the latch on the wooden door. He clipped a short chain that was hanging from a joist to the door to hold it open. "Make sure you clip the door open. It'll latch while you are in there if you aren't careful. Elizabeth had to let me out a week after we moved in."

"I'll make sure I keep it open, then," Scott said.

He peeked in through the open doorway and saw the worst infestation of spiders that he had ever seen. The dirt floor was covered with an ever changing blanket of spiders. It looked like a variety of species, which was perplexing. He would need to bomb the place, but wanted to see how much he could clear out with his spray.

"I think it'll take two or three days for the fogger to do its thing. That crawl space is cramped, but I can get in there once I clear a path. I'll put the fogger right there in the center and turn it loose. I doubt you'll ever see a spider in here again."

"That would be fantastic," Jim said.

"I'll just need you to leave me a key and I'll get started right away."

"Perfect. I've got a spare on a ring in the kitchen," he replied. He turned and led the way up the stairs.

Ten minutes later, Elizabeth and Jim pulled away from the house in their silver Jeep Cherokee. Scott waved to them and then went back inside. He wanted to spray a whole tank full of poison in the crawl space before trying to put the fogger in there.

When he got back to the small doorway in the basement, he unlatched it and clipped the little chain to hold it open, as Jim had told him to do. The spiders were still moving in waves across the dirt floor, and he felt a rush of excitement race through his body. He loved killing spiders, and this was the mother lode.

"Hasta la vista, baby," he said in his best Schwarzenegger impression and pulled his respirator over his face. He depressed the button on his spray wand and clear liquid began spraying across the crawl space. As it struck spiders, they fell dead. Others scrambled to get away from the poison, but he made a ring around the edge of the space that trapped them. He was laughing as the spray coated the floor joists, the walls, and then the floor.

Some spiders tried to come out through the small door, but slowed as soon as they touched the spray he had on the frame. They were dead seconds later. Each one spasming and then curling up into a ball. He imagined their nervous systems overloading before failing.

The sheet of spiders that had been moving across the dirt floor had stopped. A hundred or maybe a thousand of the dead or dying arachnids looked like a job well done to him. He still could not see the nest, but the fogger would only finalize the work he had already done. He made a trip back out to his van to get three blue boxes. He had them strapped together, carrying them with his right hand. His left hand held a tray with six canisters seated in it.

The first box went in the kitchen and the second in the bathroom. The canisters were inserted into small holes on the top of the boxes, but he did not activate them. He planned to do that on his way back out. His respirator would be fine for a while, but probably not more than five minutes if he got into the heaviest part of the fog.

He checked the chain on the small door and then crawled into the space below the living room. The bodies of spiders crunched under his knees and hands as he made his way across the dirt floor. The bodies of the pests smeared across his gloves and knee pads. He swept some of them out of the way with his left hand, trying to clear a path to crawl along. They were up to an inch deep in some places and he couldn't recall ever seeing anything like this before.

When he reached the center of the area, he placed the third blue box in a spot that he had cleared. The canisters slipped in easily and he was about to activate it when he heard a whistling sound. It was high-pitched and caused him to freeze on the spot. Then, he turned his head toward one of the small windows in the foundation to his right. It looked to be open, and the wind was causing the noise, so he relaxed.

That window would need to be closed, so he scooted that way and gave the wooden window three solid pulls. It didn't want to move and was the kind that pivoted out on a pair of hinges, so he had to use the two metal handles to try to close it. After the fifth pull, one of the handles broke free and sent him rolling to his side. He bumped his head on one of the joists.

"Gosh darn it!"

Finally, he did his best to grip the remaining small handle with both hands and pull. The window slipped snugly back in place, and he wondered if the spiders had started coming in through there. As he studied the window, he noticed movement out of the corner of his eye.

A dozen black spiders about the size of his palm were pushing their way up through the layer of dead spiders. They had fuzzy legs with narrow white bands. The bodies were thick and had two triangle shapes pointing toward the mouth. He was shocked by the size but believed that the nest must be down there. Six of them came up and waited, although the residue of the spray did not seem to be affecting them.

He wished he had brought the spray in with him but was sure the fogger would take care of them in minutes. He started to back away from the window and one of the spiders launched itself toward him. He was surprised by the sudden action, as it flew across the small space. He backed away instinctively, but his coveralls snagged on a stray nail in the floor joists. The spider stopped moving toward him, but he wanted to get out of there.

He reached behind his back to try to free himself from the nails but could not get his arm around there in the small space. He turned to his left to see if that would work, but it only made the situation worse. As he turned back to his right, his foot struck the fogger and knocked it to its side. The button to activate it was depressed and the fog began pouring out of the vents. He knew he had to get out, so he gave a strong pull against the nails and tore through his jumpsuit. This allowed him to crawl toward the door to the basement, although he had already started coughing. Having the fogger close to him was overpowering his respirator.

He turned around and made it three feet before realizing the door had closed. He gave it two solid shoves, but it would not budge. He wished that it had been a new, cheap door instead of the old boards on steel hinges. He should have pulled the canisters from the fogger, but that thought evaded him. Instead, he crawled straight for the window, hoping for fresh air. He was feeling weak when he got to it but started pushing anyway.

The window was jammed, and frustration overtook him. He remembered that his phone was in his pocket and started digging for it. His fingers touched the edge of the black rubber case on his phone at the moment he heard a tap and looked toward the window. The little boy he had seen earlier was staring back at him, motioning toward the window. He nodded to the boy and tried pushing, but then the corners of the boy's lips twisted up in a devilish manner. Suddenly, Scott could see him clearly. His eyes were solid black, and Scott's heart skipped a beat. The boy placed a paver against the window, effectively sealing it.

He felt delirious as the fog closed in around him. He had lost the time he needed to get his phone. He looked at the boy one last time before passing out.

Next door the boy coughed.

"Are you ok?" his mom asked.

"Yes. Can I have some water?"

"Sure. Get a clean glass out of the cabinet and wash your hands for lunch."

He scowled at his sister on his way to the kitchen.

Chapter 10

"I sure am glad I can come here when I'm feeling bad instead of going to one of those giant hospitals," Besim Sadikovic, a man in his late eighties, said in his unmistakable accent. He was a nice man, who appreciated everything the area had to offer after immigrating decades earlier to escape unrest in Bosnia. He stretched his legs in his seat at a consultation window at the Johnstown Health Clinic, waiting on his paperwork.

"Well, we are glad you came to see us, Besim," Paige Barns, a medical clerk in her early thirties, replied.

"I wonder why they don't have more places like this around the area," he asked. He lived alone, so he was happy to have someone to chat with for a while.

"We were ahead of our time, but I've heard there are a half-dozen more planned in Johnstown in the next year. The big healthcare groups are calling them Urgent Care clinics."

"Urgent Care, hmm."

"Don't get any ideas about leaving us, though."

"Never, my dear," he said. "Besides, few of my visits are urgent."

"Good," Paige said, sliding some papers across the desk to him. "Everything looks good, but don't push yourself too hard on those walks at the Commons with those Silver Striders."

"I'm only going five days a week now and I'm no speed demon."

"Yes, but the doctor thinks five might be too much. Just consider doing less on each trip. Especially if you continue to have trouble breathing."

"Okay, okay," he said. "You sound like my mother."

Paige could only shake her head. She liked Besim and was always relieved to have a patient that was pleasant. She went around the desk to help him stand up.

"Now, you have a good day, Besim," she said.

"Can't get any better than talking with you," he said and turned toward the door.

She watched him go and considered how much he reminded her of her grandpa, but her thoughts were interrupted when the double doors at the front of the waiting area slid open.

A man of about fifty with brown hair and a gray Giorgio Armani suit strode into the room, talking loudly into a Bluetooth earpiece.

"Yes, sure, yes," he said, looking around the room. "I'll be there in twenty minutes. No, there are only about ten people here and I'll just jump the line. It's good to be important."

People who were sitting in the bank of chairs on the right side of the waiting room glanced up from their magazines and phones. One older woman shook her head at him and went back to playing solitaire on her Kindle. Paige walked back to her spot behind the desk.

"Relax!" the man on the phone said. "I'm going to get this flu shot really quick so that I can get my wife off my back. Then, I'll be over. I've gotta go."

"Good morning," Paige said, forcing herself to smile. She had heard his comments clearly and was not looking forward to dealing with this one.

"Yeah, hey, I need to get my flu shot really quick."

"We can certainly get that shot for you, but the current wait time is about forty minutes. As you can see there are…"

"Stop right there," he said, waving his right hand. "You obviously don't know who I am."

"No, sir, I don't. However, the clinic serves patients in the order that they arrive."

"That's no good," he said with an angry look forming on his face. "My name is Gary Windel. I am the lead counsel for the city of Johnstown, and I have a meeting with Mayor Westchester in fifteen minutes. It is important that I get that shot immediately. I simply do not have time to wait around."

"I'm sorry, there is no way we can take care of you that quickly," she answered, staying as calm as possible. "We are open until 8 this evening, so perhaps you can stop back in after your meeting."

"You think I have time to come back? Watch this. I'll show you how this is done."

Paige watched as he took out his phone and made a call.

"Good morning, Ms. Hoffman," he said, staring directly at Paige. He enjoyed the look of disbelief on her face upon hearing the name, believing that getting the director of the clinic on the phone so quickly had to be impressive to her. "No, I wasn't calling about the financial request you put before the city council, but that will be coming up soon. I'd be happy to put in a good word for you with the mayor when I meet with him today. That's where I'm having a slight hang up. I'm trying to get my flu shot here at the clinic, but apparently the line is too long to get me in before I head over to city hall."

He paused and smiled at Paige, which gave her a creepy chill.

"Can you do that for me? That would be great. Thank you, Ms. Hoffman."

He tapped his earpiece to end the call and waited, but not long. The phone on the consultation desk gave two quick rings, signaling that it was an internal call.

"This is Paige," she said, still watching the smirking attorney. "Yes, ma'am, I'll get him right in."

She wanted to punch him in the face and her face showed it. Instead, she pulled up the paperwork needed to give a flu shot. She hit print, waited for the paper to pop out, and then slid it across the desk.

"Fill out the boxes highlighted in yellow and bring it back up. I'll have Nurse Braun prep your shot."

"Thank you so much. I'm glad we were able to work this out so quickly."

Paige wanted to tell him exactly what was on her mind but knew it would do no good. Now she only wanted to get him out of the building and apologize to all the others who had been patiently waiting their turn.

"Here you are," the attorney said when he finished filling out his paperwork.

"Thank you," Paige said in a flat tone. "Please go back to Exam Room 2 and the nurse will be right in."

"Excellent!" he said and rapped his knuckles on the desk.

He walked along the short hallway to his left and stopped at the room with a large, green 2 on the door. It was about the size of his head, which he found amusing. He saw a nurse going into the third exam room and gave her a quick smile.

"Go on in and have a seat," she said. "I'll be there in just a moment."

He stepped through the doorway and had a seat on the tan plastic chair along the wall opposite the examination table. He looked around at the various posters, showing what lungs and the heart looked like on the inside. He wondered how anyone got out of junior high without knowing those things. The chart on the side of the cabinet to his right said BMI on it and he could only laugh at the fact that it said he was obese, when he knew his body fat was under four percent. The rattling of a clipboard in the bin on the door drew his attention.

"Please remove your jacket and shirt, so I can get to your upper arm. I'll also need you to sit up on the exam table, Mr. Windel," the nurse said. "It'll be just a moment. I know you are in a hurry. I have to go back and get the shot."

"Very good," he said, looking proud. He hung up his jacket and smoothed it out, before removing and draping his shirt over the chair. Finally, he moved to the table, as instructed. The thin paper sheet covering the vinyl surface crinkled as he sat down. It made him think back to when he was a kid and loved squirming around on similar paper to drive his mother crazy.

Thirty seconds later, the nurse returned. She had a clipboard in her right hand and a sealed package in her left.

"Well now, that's service," he said. She did not respond, instead walking over to the counter. She had her back to him, but quickly opened the package with the needle in it and removed the seal on the vial with the vaccine in it. She took a Band-Aid and a piece of gauze from the cabinet and placed it next to the syringe. He beamed with joy, thinking that this prompt attention was more than he had expected. He was important.

When she turned around, she had the syringe and other supplies in her hand. He realized that it was not the nurse that had just stopped in, but the woman from the front desk. He was surprised because he did not realize she had been a nurse, thinking she was only a receptionist.

"Hey, sorry about pulling rank earlier," he said. "I'm under a lot of pressure and just trying to do what I can to get things done."

She only nodded and put the Band-Aid and gauze on the table next to him.

"I know I look tough, but I don't like needles at all. If it's ok, I'll turn my head and power through. I haven't passed out from an injection in quite a while," he said, hoping to get a laugh. Instead, she continued working without saying anything. "Just give me a heads up when you are about ready to stick me."

When she looked up, he froze in place. She was looking directly into his eyes, but all he could see was solid black where her eyes should have been. He started to scoot away, but her left hand grabbed his forearm, and he felt a sense of numbness wash over him. She was still staring at him, and he relaxed, although it was against his will.

Her right hand came up and he saw the syringe, only he realized that she had not put the medicine in it. Instead, it was full of air. He attempted to yell for help but could only manage the tiniest of squeaks. He began to tilt to his side as his muscles continued to relax. Moments later, his head reached the pillow at the top of the bed. He still couldn't take his eyes off the thing in front of him.

She brought the needle toward his neck and slipped it into his carotid artery. He twitched but could not fight back. She pushed the plunger, sending over one hundred milliliters of air into his system. The syringe was much too large for the injection he was due to receive, and he wasn't sure why he did not notice it before. However, that concern left him seconds later as he felt the pressure building in his brain.

She let go of him and the numbness started to fade instantly. He wanted to yell, but the pressure building in his head was excruciating and he could only focus on that pain. Just before passing out, he grabbed her wrist and squeezed.

A minute later, Nurse Braun passed by the reception desk. Paige was filling out some papers.

"Ow!" Paige said, looking down at her left wrist.

"What's wrong?" the nurse asked.

Paige was staring at what appeared to be deep bruises forming before her eyes. It looked like fingers wrapped around her arm.

Chapter 11

"You gonna eat that biscuit?" Willnow asked, pointing at the last biscuit in the box between he and Elliott. "I think I've only had two."

"We started with six and I've had one, so you do the math, big fella," Elliott said with a wry smile.

"Maybe you're right. It only feels like two, though."

Elliott's phone began to vibrate and dance across their table at Los Pollos Hermanos, one of the best chicken places in the West County area. It had been part of a chain at one point, but a major drug bust had brought an end to the parent company. Some franchise stores stayed open after negotiating to keep the name.

"Elliott," she said after tapping her phone. Willnow gestured at the biscuit again, so she picked it up and tossed it on his plate. He was pleased with himself. She could only shake her head.

"Elliott, this is Zinyemba. I just got a call that the morgue is filling up and the medical examiner has been working overtime."

"Is she done?"

"I think so, barring some other turn of events. Good ol' Jamie, always aiming to please."

"*Doctor* Cox is an excellent ME. I think we are lucky to have her."

"No doubt about that."

"And she's only thirty-five. That's hardly old."

"Easy, Detective. I was joking around. Anyway, I'm heading over to the morgue in about thirty minutes. Officially, I'll be there to see the report on my guy from the Quarter Bar, but..."

"I hear ya," Elliott said. "We've got a lot to look at and I'd be happy to have your input on whatever Doctor Cox came up with."

"And I would be glad to assist," Zinyemba said. "Are you at HQ right now?"

"No, Willnow and I are finishing up lunch at Los Pollos Hermanos."

"That's some good chicken. Tell Willnow not to eat more than half a bird."

"Too late," Elliott said, looking at her former partner. "He just tackled the last leg."

"Then you might want to leave him outside the exam room. I have a feeling this could be an ugly visit."

"Got it," she said. "I'll see you in a bit."

The medical examiner position for the city of Johnstown was technically only a part-time gig, but Doctor Cox had been putting in full-time hours. Adding a body every other day and then the skeleton that the contractor had found, was pushing her to the limit. There was only one tray left in the morgue, so she really hoped this rash of deaths would stop.

Twenty minutes later, Elliott found Zinyemba waiting at the bottom of the stairs leading down to the morgue. His pending mischief was plain to see on his face as he leaned against the wall with his arms crossed.

"Where'd you leave Willnow?"

"We had three leads come in from people who might 'know something' about what's going on," Elliott offered sarcastically. "Willnow said he'd rather go talk to them than come down here."

"Smart choice on his part."

"Why are morgues always in basements?"

"Have you been to a lot of morgues?" he asked.

"Luckily, no, but the ones on TV are usually tucked away in some spooky location."

"Spooky," Zinyemba said, suppressing a laugh. "The stuff on television certainly doesn't touch what we are about to look at. I can promise you that."

"Sounds great," Elliott said, shaking her head. "Let's get started."

A single steel door served as the front entrance to the morgue. 'CITY MORGUE' was stenciled in large letters on the frosted glass window that made up the top half of the door. 'Dr. J. Cox, Medical Examiner' was written in small text at the bottom of the window.

"Age before beauty," Elliott said as she pulled the door open, gesturing for Zinyemba to go in.

"Wow," he said and went in.

"Welcome, Detectives," the doctor said from the back of the long room. She wore a white cloth gown that bore fresh blood stains, making it look like she had just done a messy autopsy. An extra wide, plastic shield covered her face while her hair, hands, and feet were protected by matching teal pieces. She looked like something straight out of a TV show to Zinyemba.

"How are things down here, today?" Elliott asked.

"Oh, just peachy," Cox said. "If you all can figure out who is committing these murders and filling up my morgue, I'd appreciate it."

"We haven't ruled them as homicides, yet," Zinyemba said.

"Well, they weren't accidents and not suicides, but I'll leave the paperwork up to you, Detective."

"Thank you, Doctor Cox. I think…"

"Let's just focus on the remains from the well, shall we?" Elliott said. She didn't want to waste time on these two pretending to hash out details of things no one understood. "That's why we're here."

"Right," Cox said. She placed the tools she had been holding on the metal examination table in front of her and walked toward another table draped with a white sheet. "This is the one."

Elliott and Zinyemba cut between a pair of tables to meet the doctor, as she pulled back the sheet. The remains had been placed in the proper order with every major bone accounted for. The surface of the bones was stained a light green color.

"Why is it green?" Zinyemba asked.

"The real thing to question is that it's surprisingly good condition," Cox said. "I'm assuming the color is from the water at the bottom of that well. Who knows how long it has been sealed up in there and it's probably some sort of mildew or mold."

"Were you able to determine the cause of death?"

"Looks like trauma to the head and maybe some cracked ribs, but that's mostly my speculation. I mean, this guy could have fallen in by accident or maybe he was dropped in there. I can't even tell how old they are exactly, but they've been down there a long time. That house has been there for many years and the well was under part of it."

"How long have you had these remains?"

"Two days. I had them bagged and put in one of the lockers twice, but people have been down to look at them and I got tired of moving them."

"What people?"

"Two reporters came in yesterday. Mayor Westchester has been down here three times. He seems to think there is some sort of historical significance. He's really leaning into the theory that this could be one of his family members and that was one of his big campaign strategies. I've been busy, so I didn't pay much attention to him. However, I'm sure I heard him talking to it."

"Talking to it?" Zinyemba said with a smirk on his face.

"Yes, but he's the mayor and I have a budget increase request in front of the city council next month. Therefore, he can talk to a skeleton if he wants."

"I can appreciate that," Elliott said. "Do you expect him back?"

"I didn't expect him at all, but I'll be putting these back in storage to clear the table in case we get another unfortunate visitor in the next few days."

"We'll do our best to stop that from happening," Elliott said.

"Have I mentioned how great that would be?" Cox asked.

Chapter 12

Elliott sat at her desk, staring at the notes she had taken at each of her stops. Nothing made sense. It was like an invisible line connected each event, but it failed to follow any sort of logic. Her coffee had gone cold and a fat, black fly sat on her cake donut, but she didn't care.

"Hey," Zinyemba said, walking through the doorway.

"Why did I sign up for this job again?"

"We all have tough cases. You'll be fine."

"You've had a case like this?"

"No, but I'm trying to be supportive."

Elliott glanced up at him, swatted the fly away, and grabbed the donut. She studied it for a moment, looking for the best bite and took it. Zinyemba raised his eyebrows, seeing the desperation in her eyes. She took another bite and looked like Cookie Monster demolishing the donut.

"You might want to slow down on that. If you choke to death, I'll have to finish this case. I don't want that."

"Thanks for your concern," she said, after taking a swig of coffee to wash the food down.

"I think the skeleton is a distraction from the real problems here. I mean, the mayor wants to get the development of the bank going, so he needs the remains to be accounted for. He'll stay on you to get that pushed through."

"He hasn't said a word about that, yet."

"Really?"

"Nope. I debated that in my head over a beer last night after thinking about the morgue for an hour. Now we have the city attorney on a slab, too. It's out of control and the chief has already called me twice today."

"I wish I had some help or even a suggestion."

"I wish that, too, Z."

"Z?"

"Yeah. It's my new nickname for you."

"Since when?"

"Five seconds ago," she said. "Anyway, I need to go talk to the receptionist at the clinic. She complained of a pain after the lawyer died, which matches the other murders. However, she was definitely not in the room with him."

"I'll go do the interview for you, if you want," Zinyemba said."

"That'd be great. I'm betting she will have the same story as the bartender," she replied as her phone gave a double ring. "Ugh. The duty officer. Another murder?"

"I hope not!"

"Elliott," she said into the phone. "Yeah, send him back."

"Who is it?"

"Some guy who thinks he has a lead on my case."

"Mind if I hang out?"

"Please do. If I start to lose my temper, you can calm me down."

"I'll do my best," he said as the duty officer appeared at the doorway. He knocked.

"Detectives, I've got Joe Flaugher here..."

"Yep, send him in," Elliott said, feeling her blood pressure rising. The officer had told her the exact same thing on the phone and she wanted to get on with it.

"Oh, hi," Flaugher said, looking from Elliott to Zinyemba and back. "I didn't know there would be two of you."

"Detective Zinyemba is helping me on this case," she said, fighting the urge to roll her eyes. "What do you have for us?"

"I, well, I wanted to tell you about a connection I found between the victims," he said before pausing to push up his glasses and shift his black leather briefcase from his right hand to his left. "I think it might be helpful."

"Right, that's why you're here," Zinyemba said. "You're trying to help. Now, what do you have for us?"

"Can I set up my laptop for you?"

"Sure," Elliot said, gesturing to the small side table along the wall to the right of her desk. Zinyemba stepped over and picked up the empty Krispy Kreme box, wondering if she had eaten the whole dozen.

"Ok," Flaugher said. "Let me get connected to the Wi-Fi. What's the password?"

"Use the one named JPDPublic and you won't need one," Zinyemba answered.

"Oh, the public ones are always so slow," he replied and looked over his shoulder, hoping they would give him access to the private Wi-Fi. They did not. "Might just take an extra minute, then."

"Fine," Elliott said. "Can you tell us what we're about to look at? Our time is in high demand."

"Yes. Sure. Of course," Flaugher said while clicking through some things on his desktop. "I have a side gig. Some might call it a hobby, but it's more than that to me. It doesn't pay, really, but I don't have many expenses. Not sure if that makes it a hobby or not."

"What is this side gig?" Zinyemba asked.

"Oh, right," Flaugher said. He turned and faced them with a pleased look on his face. "You see, I'm a genealogist."

The detectives waited for a moment for him to continue, but he waited to be prodded. Elliott said, "And?"

"Well, my great great grandfather was none other than, if you can believe it, John Westchester!" He waited for a reaction, but realized he wasn't going to get one. "I found that out when I was in Junior High and started researching. Since then, I've found a lot of his descendants. He founded Johnstown, you know?"

"Yes," Zinyemba said, "we know who John Westchester was. It would be hard not to with our current Mayor Westchester using that as his primary campaign platform."

"Oh, of course, I was actually hired to confirm his claim back when he entered the race!"

"Someone hired you to figure that out? Seems odd, doesn't it?" Zinyemba asked.

"Not really," Flaugher said. "In fact, lots of people are curious about their family trees. I'm happy to help… for a nominal fee."

"Right," Elliott said. "That's why it's a side gig."

"Exactly," he said, now smiling even bigger. "So, if you want to come over and look at my computer, you'll see the John Westchester family tree."

"What does the family tree have to do with our case?" Elliott asked, still seated at her desk.

"That's the best part of all this. Maybe the worst? I don't know," he said, suddenly looking serious. "After the fourth murder or death or whatever you are calling them, one of the names caught my attention. Sarah Wilson was her name. The bank manager."

"I know who you are talking about," Elliott said, her voice raised a bit. Flaugher's eyes went wide with a look of fear.

"Detective Elliott is under a lot of pressure right now," Zinyemba said, offering a smile to Flaugher. "Please forgive her short temper. We are actually late for an interview from the site of the latest death, so, if you could cut to the core of this presentation, we would appreciate it."

"Oh, yes. Sorry. I get excited about these things sometimes and this was the biggest thing I've ever discovered."

"Sarah Wilson?" Elliott asked, trying to guide him back to the topic at hand.

"She is a descendant of John Westchester."

"So, you discovered your own cousin?" Elliott asked, starting to get up from her chair.

"Well, sort of. I didn't know she was my cousin. She's from a distant branch. I had just been working on that part of the family two days before, so the name sounded familiar."

"And that ties into our case?"

"It does!" he said, a cautious smile forming. "I opened up my Ancestry.com account and searched for her to confirm it was the same person. It was. Then, I got a crazy hunch to search for Keegan Coates. He was on another branch. Ned Clemens, the guy from the bar, was also on there, but not too far removed from Sarah."

"How many more of the victims are on your family tree project?" Elliott said, finally walking toward the laptop. She bent at the waist to get a better look.

"All of them," he answered. Both detectives turned to study him. "It is hard to believe, but I double-checked everything. It's correct. That's why I came in."

"All of the victims? But there is no evidence to tie them together," Elliott said. "Not even circumstantial."

"I don't know about any of that," Flaugher said. "I just know they were all related."

"As far as we know, they had no connection in life. Very different people," Zinyemba answered.

"How many other Johnstown residents are on that list?" Elliott asked.

"I haven't checked addresses on everyone, but there are two hundred and eleven living descendants. Well, minus the recent deaths that haven't had their cards updated."

"Close enough," Zinyemba said. "Have you checked any of them?"

"Curiosity, of course, but, yes. I found twenty-seven people who live in Johnstown on this family tree, including myself and Mayor Westchester."

"You might think about getting out of town for a week," Zinyemba said.

"It does seem like something more than a coincidence, but I have to work at my regular job until Friday. I took next week off and I'm going to visit a friend in Chicago, just in case."

"Can you leave your contact information in case we have questions?" Elliott asked.

"Gladly."

"Could you print out the family tree?" Zinyemba asked.

"Print it out? Why?"

"I work better with paper. Old school."

"Oh, well, I suppose I can. That's a lot of ink and paper, though."

"Fine," Elliott said and grabbed one of her business cards. She printed out the password for the private Wi-Fi. "Use this to access the station printers. If you use TR602, it'll come out at the front desk."

"Happy to help!" Flaugher said, believing he had reached a special level of trust that allowed him to get that password.

"We do have to get to the interview though," Elliott said. "Please print it from the lobby. I can't leave you back here unsupervised."

"As you command, Detective!"

"Thank you," Elliott said and gave a sideways glance to Zinyemba. "Can you show our guest out and I'll meet you at the car?"

Zinyemba stood up straight and saluted her. She wanted to punch him but refrained. He suppressed a laugh as she left. Flaugher missed the exchange as he rushed to pack up his computer.

Chapter 13

Tommy Wheeling had been an evening security guard at the award-winning Johnstown Zoo for twenty years on the night he volunteered to go check an alarm near the Flight Cage. There was a light fog with rain threatening from the northwest, so his coworkers Brian Pusczek and Aaron Conn were happy to let him go.

"That north door probably isn't latched right," Tommy said, clipping his walkie-talkie to his belt. He clicked his flashlight on and off to make sure it was good.

"Maybe, but it has been weeks since anyone tried hiding out after hours," Brian said. "Idiot kids think it's funny to sneak around with animals at night."

"Survival of the fittest," Aaron said without looking up from his phone.

"I don't think any of them have been dumb enough to climb in with the lions, tigers, or bears," Tommy said.

"Oh my," Aaron said.

"Wow," Tommy said. "On that note, I'm outta here."

"Check in when you get there," Brian said. "I think some of the keepers are still here, so don't get caught up chatting."

"Yeah, because you two are super busy," he said and walked out the door, making sure it clicked shut behind him.

Tommy had walked every path through the zoo at least a hundred times during his career. He often joked that he could walk from any point to another with his eyes closed. Paying attention to details had always been important to him. When he was a kid, he got lost in a theme park. That feeling of panic led him to swear he would never get lost again.

The Flight Cage didn't have a direct route to it, so he wandered down past the new bear enclosures and the carousel. He waved to the mechanic working on one of the zoo's trains, the

Ulysses S. Grant. Tommy thought the guy's name was Kenny, but he didn't ask.

"What a joke," he said when he stopped next to the 4-D ride, which was the last attraction before the Flight Cage. "Challenge your senses! Visit the land of the dinosaurs! They could have actual animals here instead of an overpriced video game."

He shook his head and walked around the corner to a steep path leading up to his destination. The South door had a sign telling visitors to be sure the outer and inner doors were not open at the same time. He gave the door a good tug and found that it was secure.

A dozen steps to his right took him along a narrow path that allowed visitors to look into the Flight Cage from outside. The giant metal dome had stood there for over a century, having once been part of the World's Fair before the zoo was built. He walked along the path, looking in at the birds. He didn't use his flashlight because that could frighten them.

As he approached the North entrance, he heard whispers. He felt his heart speed up. He wanted excitement, not another boring night. Three silhouettes stood twenty feet from the doorway.

"Hey!" he called out and aimed his flashlight in their direction. All three stopped moving for a moment and then took off up the hill ahead of him. Tommy wanted to kick himself for revealing himself too soon. Those boys would surely be faster than him. "Good thing I know this place so well. They'll probably circle the giraffe enclosure and run right back to me."

A minute later, he was panting, but had made it up the hill. The large round enclosures were mostly vacant, as the animals were usually taken inside to sleep and eat after hours. He listened for footsteps on the asphalt as he shined his light to the left, right, and back left again.

Then, he heard voices. They were something barely above a whisper, but enough to tip him off. The boys were moving toward the Reptile House. It was lucky for them that he had already locked those doors up tight.

"Where are you headed boys?" he whispered and started jogging after them. He made it to the top of the slope leading down between some of the oldest buildings in the zoo. He turned to shine his light down a narrow path going behind one of the concession stands that led to a bathroom, but the path wasn't there. "What in the world?"

He turned back to the long slope, but suddenly felt like he didn't know which way went down. He heard footsteps ahead of him but had to grab a signpost. His head was spinning, and he fought the urge to throw up.

That sensation passed after a minute, but he still felt confused. It made no sense to be lost, but things didn't match up to what he knew. He would have to set his pride aside and call in for help. He put his flashlight in the clip on his left hip and took out his radio.

"Hey, Brian or Aaron, I need assistance," he said and released the button on his walkie-talkie. He got no response. "Brian or Aaron! You guys need to turn down the TV and get back to work."

They did not respond, which was unusual, even if they were messing with him. He glanced at the walkie-talkie and realized the little red light on top wasn't lit.

"I'm an idiot," he said, turning the volume knob. It didn't click, instead it turned freely. The battery was dead, which made no sense. He had just put in a fresh one at the start of his shift and they would normally last four shifts. "That sucks."

He heard laughing behind him and he spun around, sliding the useless walkie-talkie back into its holster. He turned the flashlight back on and passed its beam over the concession stand and its picnic tables.

"Big Cat Country," he said to himself. "That's what's over there. I'm positive."

He didn't feel confident though, but he still went that way. There was a slight bend in the path, and he saw a concrete bridge to his right. Going left would take him back to the giraffes, zebras, and other such animals. He stopped moving and listened again, turning off his light.

A loud pop came from somewhere far to his right. The few lights still on at night went dark. He assumed the boys had found the electrical panels back behind the leopards. He started up the concrete bridge and clicked his flashlight on again, only it didn't turn on.

"You've got to be kidding me," he said and smacked it on his palm twice. The flashlight didn't come back on again. He looked up into the pitch-black night, trying to see any hint of which way he was going. Absolute disorientation had taken over by that point and the sweat started beading up on his forehead. "No way am I lost. Just calm down and get back to the office. Forget the boys."

He grabbed the metal rail at the side of the bridge and started walking. It had dew on it, which felt oddly cold as his hand slid along. The moon came out from behind a cloud, and he glanced down, hoping to get his bearings. He expected to see the panther enclosures, but instead saw the little pond that the tigers often relaxed in. He turned around to try and make sense of it, but the moon disappeared again.

"What's happening?" he asked himself. The uneasy sound in his voice was impossible to miss. "Get it together, man."

Tommy started walking again, feeling like he was going up, which meant he would get to those electrical panels before long and he could turn the lights back on. Finally, he reached the top of the ramp and knew he had to let go of the railing. There should be a path to his left, right, and straight ahead. The panels were ahead of him.

He started forward with his hands out ahead of him. He figured it would be about twenty-five steps to the railing beyond the leopards, then a right turn down a curved path to the little shed with the panels inside.

"I'm going to get out of this," Tommy said, as his hands touched a post that shouldn't have been there. "What is this?"

He tapped the post and wondered if it was part of the canopy between the leopards and tigers, but that would mean he turned left. It made no sense. He took a step back from the post.

A low growl came from his left and it made the hairs stand up on his neck. It sounded like a leopard that was about to strike. He was being hunted. The giant steel mesh that looked like a tent would protect him, but nothing else was working right at that point.

The moon sent a beam of light down through the clouds and landed directly on the leopards. The one he had heard growling was at the top of a tree and only about ten feet away. Its eyes locked on him. They were solid black. Tommy took a deep breath but was relieved to see that the cage was intact. The moon disappeared.

The leopard let out an angry roar and he heard the tree move. The big cat slammed against the steel cage and Tommy stumbled backward in a reflexive retreat. He tripped over a seam in the concrete, when he tried to turn around. He flailed, hoping to balance himself, but felt nothing.

Instead, he slammed into the railing over the tiger enclosure and managed to grab on. His upper body tipped forward, but he would have been okay. The problem was that he felt two cold hands press into his back and shove.

As he looked down, he saw that he wasn't over the tiger enclosure. Instead, he was over the entrance to one of the train tunnels. His hands slipped off the dewy railing and he went down. The fall happened in slow motion to him, right up to the point where his head struck one of the large pieces of rip rap over the tunnel. His neck snapped and his body crumpled onto the tracks below.

The shadowy figure near the railing dissipated like fog in a breeze. Aaron and Brian would find his body about thirty minutes later when they finished their show and realized Tommy hadn't checked in. Detective Elliott got the call less than an hour after he died.

Chapter 14

"I'm exhausted," Elliott said, as she slid into the passenger seat of Zinyemba's car. She hadn't been able to sleep after getting the call about Tommy Wheeling the night before. "How do you do this?"

"Do what?"

"Handle being a detective. You've been doing it forever and somehow you don't look like a partially resuscitated cadaver. That's how I would describe my appearance today," she said, giving her messy bun a shake.

"Two things," Zinyemba said. "One, I have had exactly zero murder cases. You've got them piling up every day. We're in this together. Two, your hair looks fine. Those bags under your eyes though."

She shot him a look and he offered a slight smile. He backed out of his parking space and started out of the lot. A uniformed officer walked out of the building waving at them.

"What now?" Zinyemba said, rolling down his window.

"The mayor just called," the officer said.

"Fantastic."

"He wants both of you to meet him at the morgue."

"People in hell want ice water," Zinyemba said.

"He's already there."

"Thanks, we'll head over there shortly."

"I mean, okay, but he's waiting."

"He can keep waiting," Zinyemba said. He smirked. "No, don't go telling him that. We will head over there after a stop at QT."

"Alright. If he calls back, I'll let him know you're on the way," the officer said. "He makes me nervous and he's the mayor, after all."

"Mayors come and go. He's just the guy with the title right now," Zinyemba said and rolled up his window. "Now for coffee."

"And a doughnut?" Elliott asked. She had reclined the seat. Her eyes were closed.

"Can we be more stereotypical?"

"As long as it's the kind of stereotype that gives me a large, black coffee and an apple fritter."

"Sounds good to me."

Half an hour later they pulled into a spot at the morgue, right next to the mayor's truck. Elliott took a long drink of coffee and the last bite of her fritter. Zinyemba put the car in park and sat quietly.

"Should we go in?" Elliott asked, glancing in the mirror.

"He can wait five more minutes."

"I'd rather just get this over with," she said and opened her door. "We've got real work to do."

"Agreed, boss lady," he said. She only shook her head before getting out.

Zinyemba held open the front door to the building and Elliott led the way downstairs. She shifted her coffee to the other hand, so she could grab the handle to go in the morgue.

"Detective Elliott! Detective Zendaya… or whatever your name is. Thank you for coming on such short notice!" said the mayor as soon as they entered the morgue.

"What can we do for you today, Mr. Mayor?" Elliott asked.

"Straight to business!" he said in a pompous tone. "I like it. So, we have a problem with all these people dying, right?"

"I'd say that's an understatement."

"Right, right, but what about these bones? I mean, we need to know where they came from and how they got there. The progress on the building site is at a standstill until we get some answers."

"Wait," Zinyemba said. "You're wanting us to turn our attention to some bones rather than finding an active serial killer?"

"Serial killer?!"

"Yes. Haven't you been reading the reports the chief is sending you every day? The ones you specifically asked for?"

"Sure, I mean, sure. Interesting stuff," he said and turned to the tray pulled open to his left. "I just don't understand how this poor fellow ended up in that well. He probably worked with some of my relatives, you know."

"Where is Doctor Cox?" Elliott asked.

"She's in her office, I think."

"No, she's right here," Cox said, coming in from the back hallway. "The good mayor has been so interested in these remains that he's down here five or six times a day."

"That sounded sarcastic," the mayor said.

"Maybe. Normally, I don't leave anyone in here without supervision, but I've got a ton of work to do with all these murders. No offense."

"None taken," Elliott said. "So, what do you want us to do, mayor?"

"I'm not asking you to do anything special, but maybe we can do more research on this skeleton? Can we do some DNA tests? Maybe carbon dating?"

"You watch CSI a lot?" Cox asked.

"I've seen most of the episodes, I think. I'm more of a Criminal Minds fan."

"Makes sense, then," she said and raised her eyebrows while looking from Elliott to Zinyemba. "Not everything they do on the show is just that easy. Carbon dating is for things a lot older than these bones. I did do some DNA tests, though. We should have results before long."

"Excellent! I can make some phone calls and get those tests expedited."

"That won't be necessary," Cox said. "The labs work as fast as they can."

"Alright," the mayor said, turning to Elliott, "what can I do to help you two while we wait on that lab to get their work done?"

"I think we can handle it," Elliott said. "We just need time to get out and follow leads. Maybe just call next time?"

"I'm a firm believer in face to face meetings. Conveying my true passion for this situation is important to me."

"Yes, I understand how important this is to you. We will keep doing everything we can, but I need you to let us do our job."

"Of course! I would never want to get in the way," he said with a broad, fake smile.

Doctor Cox had moved over to the most recent murder victim and was looking at her notes. She had little interest in anything the mayor had to say at this point. She wanted him to stay out of her morgue.

Her phone dinged, so she picked it up and tapped on her inbox. She read the new message and shook her head.

"Well, now, isn't that convenient," she said, drawing the attention of the other three.

"What is it?" Elliot asked.

"The results from the DNA test are in."

"That is amazing news!" the mayor said, walking toward her.

"They compared the results to some other samples I sent along, and one thing is for certain," she said. "These remains are from someone related to John Westchester."

"But how?" the mayor asked. "Why would someone from our founder's family be at the bottom of that well?"

"That is well beyond the scope of my responsibilities," Cox said. "I can just tell you that he was related to the family. If we wanted to exhume John Westchester, we could see how close they are. Otherwise, we are dealing with making a good guess since the DNA has moved further away from John's with each generation."

"No, no, no," the mayor said. "We won't be exhuming the founder. He deserves better than that! Since I know that these remains are from my family, they will be treated with respect."

"Yes, of course," Elliott said. "Can we put them away now?"

"I think that's fine," Cox said.

"Of course it is," the mayor said. "I will get to work on arrangements for my ancestor. The mystery is solved."

"Now, if you don't mind, we're going to get back to solving the bigger mystery," Elliott said. "You know, the serial killer."

"Yes, good work, detectives. Please keep me up to date! I look for that report in the morning," the mayor said and walked out the door. The tapping of his dress shoes could be heard going up the stairs. The doctor crossed over to the tray of remains from the well and pushed it shut. The door clicked and she twisted the handle to seal it.

"Maybe that will keep him out of our way for a while," Zinyemba said.

"We can only hope," Elliott said. "You think he paid any attention to the fact that all the victims are related to John Westchester, just like him?"

"I doubt it," Zinyemba said. "It's not like his majesty would leave the city anyway."

"That would be his best choice, though."

"I'm not calling him," Cox said.

"Yeah," Elliott said, "let's get back to work. Thanks, Doc."

Chapter 15

"Bologna and cheese!" Joe Flaugher said as he squeezed some mayonnaise on two slices of bread. "Hard to beat that after a long day."

His cat, Paddy, sat on its little tree in the corner, staring at him. It didn't care about the sandwich, but probably wouldn't have eaten bologna anyway. Joe put on the meat and Colby Jack cheese and grabbed a bag of Cool Ranch Doritos.

"The perfect meal for doing my research," he said. He walked past the archway leading to his living room and continued down the hallway. The second door on the right was the small room he called an office.

It had been three full days since Tommy Wheeling died at the zoo. That had been declared an accident, but Joe had done his research. Wheeling was at the end of one of the branches on the Westchester family tree.

"No more killings. Seems too good to be true," he said, taking a bite out of his sandwich. He stared at the ancestry website and clicked between the branches. It was a massive project, but it was getting more and more interesting. "I think I'll make a list of the people on this tree that live in or around Johnstown. Detective Elliott might find that useful. I might even get one of those medals or a key to the city when this is solved."

He took another bite. The seal on his Mountain Dew cracked as he twisted off the cap. Saving even one life would make him feel like this work was worth it. Dealing directly with a serial killer was not his thing, though. The fact that he was on the family tree also had him worried.

"I can hardly wait for that trip to Chicago next week. Maybe I need to take a longer vacation!" he said. He glanced at the calendar on the wall. It was a freebie that he had picked up from the bank. His work schedule had been neatly written on it. "Too bad I don't have the vacation days to take. Maybe I could go on leave?"

The options cycled through his head as he chomped on Cool Ranch Doritos. The Dew washed it all down as his phone started playing the theme song from Star Trek: The Next Generation.

"Unknown Caller, huh?" he said and looked at the screen. "Eh, why not? Hello?"

"Is this Mr. Joseph Flaugher?"

"Is this a telemarketer?"

"Definitely not!" said an energetic voice on the other end of the call. "This is Mayor Jack Westchester!"

"Oh," Joe said, feeling nervous.

"Still there, friend?"

"Yes, Mr. Mayor, but please call me Joe. What can I do for you?"

"I saw in the notes from our good detectives that you offered up some help and a theory."

"They included me in their notes?" Joe said, sitting up straight. "That's really cool."

"Tell me more about this theory, Joe. You think all the victims are related?"

"No, I *know* they are related. I have the proof. I'm on the list and so are you, Mr. Mayor. Would you like to see it?"

"That's not necessary. I have faith in your research. I need you to do me a favor."

"Name it!"

"Come out to the building site with me. I'm curious about that well and would like to talk through some ideas with a real history buff."

"Go to the actual site?" Joe asked. "I don't know. It's dusk and it seems like that would be the perfect place for the serial killer to strike. Especially if there are two of us. Descendants of John Westchester, I mean."

"Precisely why we should go together! All of the other victims were alone. We just need to stick together, and we can figure this out before the detectives do."

"Seems risky."

"Think of the good we can accomplish! We'll be heroes."

"I guess so," Joe said, thinking about the list he had planned on making. "A quick trip over to the site can't hurt anything. What do we need to go there for?"

"I am a firm believer in powers beyond human comprehension. I think standing where our city's founder once stood could give us a lead. We can look out across the land that was once his."

"Can you pick me up? I ride my bicycle to work and don't really want to pedal out to your building site."

"Absolutely. Be there in fifteen minutes. I have your address from the file."

"Thanks, I just want to finish up my dinner."

"No, Joe. Thank you!"

Half an hour later, the mayor's truck stopped at the edge of the building site. The sun had set behind them, but Jack was prepared with a Maglite that could light up the entire property. The temperature was dropping as night set in, allowing for a thin layer of dew to form on the grass that hadn't been torn out by the construction crew.

"Why did we need to come out here at night?" Joe asked.

"I had a hectic day running the city but didn't want to put off this research. It's fine. I own the land."

"I wasn't worried about trespassing. Something more along the lines of two descendants of John Westchester in the same place and how that might be tempting for whoever is committing these crimes."

"You've already expressed that concern, but please," Jack said, "don't worry about that. The two of us will be fine. Besides, I have my trusty revolver with me."

"Trusty revolver?"

"I carry it with me most of the time. Being a politician can be dangerous work these days."

"Right. I guess it could be. So, what exactly are you wanting to look at?"

"Back to business!" Jack said and started walking toward where the house had been. "Follow me. I want to have a look at the well that was under the house."

"The well was under the house?"

"Yes. It's strange, but I was hoping your historical knowledge could help with figuring it out."

"I don't know that much about architecture. I work on ancestry stuff."

"Fine, but let's have a look anyway," Jack said, continuing across the torn-up land. "Watch your step. We're close."

The ruts from the big machines would have made quick work of their ankles with a misstep. Little puddles had formed at the bottom of them. Joe was focused on each step when he felt a sudden cold chill race up his arms.

"Whoa!"

"What is it?" Jack asked.

"Just a cold chill. Kinda freaked me out."

"Don't overthink this. We're going to be fine. Just don't fall in the well!" the mayor said. Joe wasn't impressed. Jack clicked the button on the Maglite and pointed it into the well ahead of them. "So, I had them check and see if anything else was down there, but they didn't find anything."

"So, there really was a skeleton down there?"

"There was, but don't worry about that. They didn't find anything else."

"Alright," Joe said, lowering himself to his knees to have a better look in the well. "Can I use your light?"

"Sure," Jack said, handing him the flashlight. Joe started shining the light along the walls, studying the bricks. They were still in good order with only a dozen or so out of place. Near the waterline, three of them looked to have crumbled and allowed the ones above it to make something close to a chevron pattern. "See anything?"

"Nothing too crazy. Can't tell how deep the water is, though. Did they check that?"

"They just said they didn't find anything. Maybe they weren't as thorough as I thought. I've got a tape measure in the truck if you want it."

"How long is it?"

"Fifty footer."

"That'll be more than enough, I think."

"Great. I'll be right back," Jack said and started off toward the truck, still being careful of the ruts. Joe kept studying the walls. He found it interesting, even though this was not in his normal line of work.

He heard footsteps come up on his left and put his hand out before he said, "Thanks."

His hand remained empty, so he turned to look at the mayor. The darkness outside of the well made him blink. He focused on Jack, but realized it wasn't the mayor at all. His body refused to move as he watched the thing in front of him bring its right hand down to punch him in the face. He tilted to the side and then a kick sent him tumbling down into the well.

His hands struck the wall and then his head took a glancing blow from one of the bricks that stood slightly out of place. When he splashed down, it drew Jack's attention. He had gotten distracted by an email on his phone but started back toward the well.

Joe scrambled to get to his feet and found that the water was only two feet deep. His head throbbed, but he tried to stand up. Just then he heard a whoosh as the thing from the top of the well jumped in feet first. Its heels struck Joe in the back, driving him down into the water.

He started to stand again but let out a yell as it brought a knee up into his jaw and delivered a vicious kick to his left rib cage. Then, the thing gave a quick jab to either side of his head. Jack was about ten feet from the edge of the well when he stepped wrong on one of the ruts. There was a pop from his right ankle, and he went down. He cried out in pain, losing track of his goal to help Joe.

Two more punches connected with Joe's face, and he felt dizzy. He reached for the wall but found nothing. Instead, he fell over and went into the water. He made an attempt to push himself up, but felt the thing step up onto his back. It was impossibly heavy, and Joe struggled in vain.

Minutes later, Jack pulled himself to the edge of the well and looked down. There was no sound. He could make out the faint glow of the Maglite under the water. As he squinted, he finally made out the edge of a body. A green gas erupted up at him and he rolled away from the well. When he opened his eyes, the sky was clear.

"I'm so sorry, Joe," he said and pulled out his phone.

"911. What is your emergency?" said the woman at the other end of Jack's call.

"This is Mayor Westchester. I need to report an accident," he said, but started believing that it wasn't an accident at all.

Chapter 16

Exhaustion had become a state of being for Elliott. Lack of sleep was bad, but being at the office was worse. There was not a room in that whole building that she could work in without having someone stop in to see how she was doing or if she had made any progress. The chief approved some time working from home.

She had her laptop on her coffee table and numerous papers spread across the glass surface. The paper files were growing every day as more people filed complaints of strange occurrences. She had documentation on eight people who had near-death experiences with something they claimed to be supernatural. Elliott located four of them on Flaugher's family tree but hadn't spent a ton of time digging through the hundreds of pages that he had assembled.

A cup of room-temperature coffee stood amongst the papers, but she had barely touched it. The death of Joe Flaugher had hit her pretty hard. His work had connected all the victims.

Her phone started vibrating on the end table to her right, where she usually charged it. The possibility of another death left her wanting to ignore the call, but she knew it was her duty to answer. She sighed and scooted over to grab the phone.

"This is Elliott," she said, sounding tired.

"Meredith? It's Jamie Cox. Are you busy?"

"I feel like I'm literally working twenty-four hours a day. Otherwise, I'm good. Please tell me I don't have another body to deal with."

"Not that I'm aware of. Actually, it's the opposite."

"What do you mean?"

"The remains from the well. They're gone."

"Gone?" Elliott asked. "How? Who would want... oh. Jack Westchester."

"I mean, yeah, it makes sense, but all I have is the surveillance footage from last night. Two pretty big guys came in with a backboard, like something you'd see them use at a soccer game. They knew exactly where to look and made quick work of the move."

"Can you see their faces? Was one of them the mayor?"

"No, the mayor wasn't with them, and they had masks on. I'd be willing to bet he's connected to it though. Each time he's been here, at the morgue, he's had some big guys with him."

"What time were they there?"

"The security system put their arrival at 5:53," Doctor Cox said. "When I said they made quick work, I was overstating it. The fact is they took close to an hour. They moved each piece of the skeleton with great care. I don't know why, though."

"They were following orders. I'm sure."

"Oh, the men were driving a black hearse. I believe it was a Lincoln. The camera outside the entrance is filthy, so I can't make out the plates. Never really bothered to look at that video feed before. Seems odd for them to have one of those sitting around."

"You're right. I'm going to make some calls and I'll let you know if I need anything else," Elliott said. "Please keep me updated if you hear of or see anything new. Oh, can you send me a copy of the video?"

"I sure will. Goodbye, Detective."

Elliott ended the call and placed the phone back on the table. She stared at it for ten minutes, trying to process what she had learned. The mayor's extreme interest in those remains makes it hard to believe he hadn't had those men steal them. She began to wonder if he had lost his mind or if he was behind the murders. She picked the phone up again and scrolled to Zinyemba's name.

"What's up?"

"Z?"

"Really? We're still doing that?"

"We've got a twist and I need you to do some digging for me," Elliott said.

"Name it."

"I need you to see if there are any black Lincoln hearses registered in Johnstown or nearby."

"Hearses? I'm sure there are dozens of them in the area. I can think of six decent sized funeral homes. Each one is sure to have at least two hearses."

"I know. It's a long shot but check for Lincolns first."

"License plate?"

"No," Elliott said, staring at a stack of papers. "Wait. See if any of them are registered to funeral homes that might have connections to the mayor."

"You think the mayor is behind this?"

"It's a guess, but I think he's got to be connected somehow. Get the full list if nothing catches your eye."

"Are you doing all right?"

"I'm exhausted and I just want this to all be over."

"Well, I think you're doing pretty well with this mess and I'm glad it isn't me."

"Wow," Elliott said, smirking. "Thanks for that."

"I'll give you a call as soon as I get the report. Give me an hour?"

"That'll do. Thanks again, Zinyemba," she said and hung up. She picked up the coffee and stared at the oily black surface before throwing back the rest of the cup. The lukewarm liquid tasted fine, and the temperature revived her. The grandfather clock her dad had given her struck noon. She grabbed her keys and headed out to start her search for the hearse.

Chapter 17

"I know, Stacey," Kristen Vincent said, as she pulled a pair of shoes out of her suitcase. "I don't want to miss any more days of school than I have to."

"The sub is atrocious. I can hear the kids from across the hall."

"Can you at least check in on them and remind them that I'll be back soon? Promise them a pizza party or something."

"You're going to supply pizza to that crowd?"

"Hey, now! Those are my kids," Kristen said, smiling to herself. "I had to come home for the funeral. You know that."

"I'm just giving you a hard time, Ms. V."

"Shut up, Stacey."

"Are you at least getting to do something to relax?"

"Yeah, I'm going to go grab lunch at a bar I went to when I was home from college."

"Sounds quaint."

"Oh, it is. Very fancy," Kristen said. "Trust me, I'll be glad to get back home. This place seems like it hasn't changed since I was a kid, other than tearing down some old houses to build a bunch of strip malls and banks."

"Fantastic. Have you been doing any writing?"

"Yeah, there isn't much else to do here, and it has kept my mind off the visitation tonight. I hate these things."

"What book are you on now?"

"Can you keep a secret?"

"Probably not."

"So honest," Kristen said. "I'll tell you anyway."

"I knew you would," Stacey answered.

"I finished *Within Her Thoughts* about an hour ago. I sent it to my editor."

"What?" Stacey yelled. "You didn't tell me you were done! I want a copy. Right now."

"I was going to go to the rec center to get some exercise, but I think I'll get drinks and lunch instead. I'll send you a link to the Google Doc as soon as I get back. Ok?"

"Do it before you get drinks."

"Yes, fine," Kristen said. "Don't you have some kids to teach?"

"I guess. Two minutes until lunch is over. No rush, right?"

"Right."

"Anyway, call me tomorrow after school. You'll be home in two days, right?"

"I might try to bump up my flight to tomorrow night."

"Cool. Have fun at your little bar or whatever. Have a beer for me and get me that book!"

"Bye!" Kristen said just before Stacey hung up.

She slipped on her shoes and grabbed her purse. Her phone dinged and she glanced over to see that her Uber was only two minutes away.

"Two drinks, some wings, and then back to the hotel to get ready," she said out loud. "Can't be tipsy in front of family."

She glanced at her laptop before heading out the door. Three clicks on her mouse and the new book was on its way to Stacey. She closed it and slid it into the case. She made sure she had her wallet and room key before walking out the door.

Three minutes later she walked out of the elevator and saw a black Honda Civic waiting. She glanced at the phone again. The app showed her driver was still a minute away, but the make of the car matched, and the Uber sign glowed on the dash.

"Elena?" Kristen asked as she got in the car. The driver gave a thumbs-up, but didn't speak. "Alrighty then. I'm going to the French Quarter."

Two miles away, they pulled into the bar's parking lot. Yellow caution tape still stretched between two posts at the back of the parking lot. The driver stopped near the patio and waited for

Kristen to get out. She hadn't said a word, which was really strange.

"Have a good one," Kristen said, closing the door behind her. "Definitely not a five star ride."

She put her thumb on her phone to unlock it. She tapped on the notification that her driver was waiting.

"She must not have clicked to start the ride. That's annoying," she said and started to click on the button for reporting an error. "I'll just…"

She never got to finish that sentence as someone rushed up behind her and grabbed her around the waist. It took her breath away as they raced toward the back of the parking lot. She threw an elbow behind her, landing a solid shot to the gut of whoever had picked her up, but it didn't faze them.

"Put me down! Right now!" she yelled. They continued around an old bus at the back of the lot and her head struck a side mirror, knocking her out.

A short while later she woke up, laying between two big trees. She looked around in a panic, not recognizing where she was. Kristen felt the ground around her, hoping to find her phone. Surprisingly, it was right next to her. She didn't see anyone and sat up.

"Help me!" she yelled into the phone as she tapped the emergency button over and over again. The phone rang twice, and a woman's voice answered. "Help me! I'm in some trees!"

"Please state your emergency," the woman said a second time. Kristen started to answer, but then saw a woman slide out from behind a tree. The hood of her black and white sweatshirt was pulled up around her face, which was too pale.

"Wait," she said, "you're the Uber driver! What are you doing?"

"Please repeat that," the dispatcher said.

"Look. I don't know what you want, but you can't just take people," she said. The woman standing before didn't move.

Kristen stared up at her, realizing that she was at least two inches taller than the driver. How could she have carried her this far away? Where were they? "If you're after extra money, you can have whatever cash is in my purse."

"Ma'am?" the dispatcher said. "What did you say?"

The woman in front of her took a slow step forward and pulled her hands out of the pocket on the front of the hoodie. Each one held a narrow knife with a blade close to six inches long. Kristen's eyes went wide.

"No! You don't have to do this. You can have whatever you want. I have a wife and two daughters! I'm a teacher. There isn't much in the wallet, but it's yours. I won't tell anyone!"

"I'm sending a car to your location now," the dispatcher said. "We've got your location at New Johnstown Park."

The hooded figure crouched. Kristen started scooting back, trying to get to her feet. The woman pounced forward like a big cat attacking its prey on a PBS show. She landed on Kristen's lap and pushed her back against the ground.

The first blade sank into Kristen's abdomen as she started to beg again. Her words never came out, but a bubble of blood burst through her gritted teeth. Her eyes studied the solid black surface where the woman's eyes should have been. Her mind raced to her wife and kids. Her best friend and fellow teacher, Stacey, at school along with her students came next.

The second blade felt cold against her throat as she started to cry. Her body felt numb, although she wanted to fight back. Then the sharp pain of the blade slicing through her neck registered. She coughed again and sprayed blood onto the figure.

Halfway across Johnstown, the driver of the Civic hit a pothole. She realized that she hadn't started Kristen's ride until after she got out at the bar. She was pissed because that meant she wouldn't get paid.

She went offline and pulled in to get a strawberry smoothie at a local place. She had taken her first drink as she pulled out onto the road and hit a pothole. The cup slipped from her hand and the pink smoothie splattered on her black sweatshirt. She cursed the bad luck and pulled off into a parking lot.

Chapter 18

"I know it's not what you want to hear, but I think that's what's happening," Elliott said after debriefing Chief McMahon. He had a cup of coffee in his left hand but sat still. She started to feel uneasy because he wasn't responding. That was unusual for him. "Chief?"

"Damn it!" he yelled and threw his coffee across the office. The paper cup mashed against a cabinet door. Coffee sprayed up along the door and onto the wall. Elliott ducked to her right as a reflex but didn't think the chief was trying to hit her. "That son of a bitch. He sat in here talking about needing my help and then he does this."

"I don't think he knew it was a relative until yesterday."

"I don't care who the remains are from. I let that jackass sway my better judgment because of his position. I've never done that with any other mayor. He sent guys to the morgue to flat out steal evidence from an investigation!"

"Don't be too hard on yourself, Chief. We'll figure it out."

"Damn right, we will! What do you need?" McMahon said, looking Elliott square in the eyes.

Eight officers were called in over the next hour to work in pairs. Their instructions were to find a black hearse matching the description given by Detective Elliott. No traffic stops, no answering calls, just searching. Each pair was given an unmarked car and went out in plain clothes.

Officers Schmidt and McEachron pulled into a spot at the back of the Starbucks parking lot across the road from the lot where the Westchester house had once stood. Schmidt put the car in park and let out a sigh.

"What?" McEachron asked.

"I'm bored. Glad to get the overtime, but this isn't what I had in mind for the weekend."

"Police work doesn't fit your schedule? Poor baby."

"Shut up. Let's get coffee," Schmidt said. "I want to go in so I can stand up for a minute."

"I'm good with that," McEachron said as her phone started ringing. "It's Elliott."

"I'll be inside."

"No, stay put," she said. "What's up, Red?"

"Did Willnow tell you to call me that?" Elliott said, suppressing a laugh. "Got an update for me?"

"Hey," Schmidt said. "We've only been at this for six hours. Don't rush us!"

"Tell that to the people in the morgue."

"Wow. Buzzkill."

"For real, though. Are you two wearing matching fanny packs today?"

"No," McEachron said. "We aren't even wearing fanny packs today. Matching blue shirts? Yes."

"Are you wearing your sidearms?"

"Yes."

"So, matching blue shirts with jeans that are probably about the same. I know you have matching holsters and I bet both of you are wearing your boots with a recent polish?"

"Maybe."

"You are supposed to be in plain clothes so that you don't look like cops, but I don't think you'd look any more like cops unless you were in uniform."

"Look, Mom," Schmidt said, "we're just trying to find these guys and their hearse. Can we get back to it?"

"Getting coffee first?"

"What?" McEachron asked.

"I'm sitting about fifty feet behind you. Late lunch at Texas Roadhouse with the chief."

"Seriously? You get free lunch while we're out here driving around?"

"Want to trade?"

"Not a chance," Schmidt said. Elliott rolled up right next to them and stopped. Their windows went down, and Elliott hung up.

"Bad luck for me. Give me a call if you find anything or if you happen to see the mayor."

"Will do," McEachron said and glanced at Schmidt, who nodded. They turned back to Elliott. They both made circles with their thumbs and forefingers before turning their hands upside down to put them over their eyes.

"We'll have our binoculars on, Detective."

"You two are a mess. I'm leaving," Elliott said and started forward, but immediately stopped. "Seriously though, thanks for helping out today."

"Glad to do it," McEachron said, still wearing her finger binoculars. Elliott shook her head and pulled away. "Are you ready to grab those coffees?"

Schmidt didn't respond, so she turned to look at her. The finger binoculars were gone, but she focused across the parking lot and into the collection of ball fields behind the row of businesses. A white truck sat alongside a storage building with a black sedan parked next to it.

"Is that the mayor's truck?" Schmidt asked.

"Can't tell. Maybe? Want to head over there?"

"No way. If he spots us, he'll shut down anything he's got going today."

"Good point. Let's watch the car. Probably some of his lackeys."

"So, no coffee?" Schmidt asked.

"Yeah, you go in and get it. If they take off, I'll follow them and send Elliott to pick you up."

"Works for me," she said and opened the door.

"Shut the damn door!" McEachron said and started laughing.

"I want coffee, though."

"Just have to wait until we see if this pans out."

"Think they deliver to the parking lot?"

"You're ridiculous."

"But you love me," Schmidt said, batting her lashes.

"Don't push it," she replied and looked back at the truck and car.

Light traffic went in and out of the ballfield entrance. The headlights came to life on the white truck, and it eased back behind the building. They couldn't see where it went. The car backed into the lane leaving that lot and drove out to the feeder road. Schmidt started the car.

"See if you can get the plates on it," she said.

The car drove about a hundred feet at a casual pace before turning left into a parking spot in front of the building that had housed San Clemente Flooring and Tile until three months before the murders had started. Paper had been put up over the windows and a construction permit was taped to the front door.

"What are they putting in there?"

"No clue. Want me to find out? Elliott can make a call."

"Let's see what happens first," McEachron said. About that time a guy that looked like a bouncer at the club she used to go to got out of the car. He walked to the corner of the building and let out a groan when he knelt to tie his shoe.

"Call it in," Schmidt said and reached for the handle to open her door.

"Why? He's tying his shoe."

"That fool is wearing Crocs. You go to the back of the coffee shop, and I'll circle around the other way to come in behind him."

"Got it."

The man looked to his left, right, and behind him. He stood up and dusted off his pants before walking along a narrow sidewalk leading to the back of the building.

"What's back there?" Schmidt asked.

"I think some old guy had a computer repair shop back there maybe ten years ago. My dad had him do some work for us when I was in high school."

"High School? You said ten years ago."

"Shut up."

"Alright. Once he's out of sight, move so you can see down that walkway. I'm going to follow him in."

"That's a terrible plan. Let's wait for backup."

"I just want to keep eyes on him. One of the other teams and probably Elliott will be here soon."

"Fine but be careful."

"Ok, Mom," Schmidt said and got out. She walked directly to her left, going toward the box store nearest the end of the parking lot. Her plan was to go around the opposite side of the former flooring store and try to get a peek at the guy.

McEachron took her spot next to the dumpster enclosure at the back of the coffee shop. She could see most of the way down the walkway the suspect had used. She watched her partner go to the front door of the store ahead of her before cutting down a grassy embankment and across the street. She lost sight of Schmidt when she went behind the flooring building.

"I don't like this at all," she said to herself and crept forward, watching for the man to come back along the walkway. She had one hand on her weapon and the other gripped her phone. Elliott's number was queued up.

Schmidt saw that there were no windows on the left side of the building, other than those set into a pair of roll-up doors. One of the doors served a small loading dock that was about four feet deep. The other was at ground level. She kept moving but ducked down as she got to the back of what had been the computer shop. Three windows faced a concrete retaining wall, but there was still room to walk along the rear of the building.

She looked through the first window and saw the big man kicked back in a desk chair. There were shelves with computer parts along the far wall. He was looking in that direction while talking on the phone. Moving to the second and then the third window, she noticed that a narrow door stood open. She was sure it had to lead into the flooring building.

"Look, man, he just said we gotta get everything ready for tonight," the big guy said to the person on the other end of his call. "Yeah, it's weird, but it pays the bills. I have the candelabras set up and I rolled out some blue carpet in front of the casket. I need you to bring some folding chairs and some flowers."

Schmidt listened through the cheap windows. She started typing a text to McEachron. It said, "Planning for a funeral. Makes no sense unless the mayor has completely lost his mind."

She finished typing and looked up to lock eyes with the big guy. He had stopped talking, but only swiveled in his chair. He jumped up faster than she thought he would have been able to, but she was still quicker. Bolting down the walkway, she got a good head start on him. She ran straight across the street, up the embankment, and slid in behind a minivan.

McEachron moved along the row of cars to back up her partner, watching for the big man. He did not make her wait long. He trotted to a stop next to his car and scanned the area. Luckily, Schmidt had avoided giving him a full view. He only knew she had dark, wavy hair.

He started across the street after waiting on a red pickup. When he got to the top of the embankment, he studied the lot, but finally pulled out his phone. There were simply too many people moving around the lot to try to look for her. He turned to walk back across the street, as McEachron moved to Schmidt.

"You good?"

"Yeah. What's he doing?"

"He's going back."

"Good. Call Elliott. Tell her to get here right away."

"Is this the place?"

"I'd say it's worth a look. She's going to need a warrant, though. If the mayor is involved, that could be a challenge," Schmidt said, catching her breath.

McEachron pressed call on her phone and waited for Elliott to answer.

Chapter 19

Barely a mile away from the flooring store, Mayor Jack Westchester sat at his desk. His office occupied one of the corners of the fifth floor of city hall. The walls were glass and windows stretched from floor to ceiling. His desk faced the door, but he often sat looking out the windows at his city. Subdivisions stretched out before him to his left and a strip of box stores stood to his right.

He was watching some workers load plywood onto a flatbed truck across the street at Lowe's when his phone rang. He saw the number and felt the heat rise up his neck.

Jack answered and said, "What now, Benny? It hasn't been five minutes since we met, so I know you haven't finished the task."

"No, everything will be set up soon, but…"

"Then, what is it?"

"I was on the phone with Sal, and I saw a woman out the window. Looked her straight in the eye."

"Which window?"

"I was sitting in the computer room on the phone, turned around, and there she was. Right out the back window."

"Who was it?"

"How should I know? All I caught was curly or wavy hair. Looked pretty long."

"What else?" Jack said. He got to his feet, concerned that his plan had been jeopardized. "Did she follow you there?"

"No, no one followed me. I went strictly by your instructions when I got here."

"Fine. Make sure you check all the windows for proper covering and close that door leading through from the computer room. I don't want anyone getting a peek."

"I'll call Sal back and get things together. We'll be ready for tonight."

"You do that. I'll be there in an hour. I'm going to run home, get changed, and stop off for the items I want for the service. I want you to be ready when I get there."

"We will be ready, sir."

"I know you will," Jack said and ended the call. He stared out at the workers again. A thin smile formed across his face. The woman was probably just another person being nosy and got spooked when she saw his guy. "I think a well-aged bottle of red would serve well for this occasion. They will have the flower arrangements, but I think I'll pick up a special bouquet of my own."

He slipped his laptop into the leather bag on the floor next to him. His phone went into his left pants pocket. He tapped the intercom and said, "Ashley?"

"Yes, Mayor Westchester."

"I'm taking off early today. I have a special meeting tonight."

"Very good, sir, but I don't see it on your schedule."

"No, it's a personal matter."

"Ok. I'll see you tomorrow, then. Have a good evening, sir."

"I will," he said and clicked the intercom off.

Five minutes later, he made his way along the back hallway that allowed him to get from his office to the elevator at the back of the building. It wasn't open to the public, which made it the only way he would leave the building unless he was putting on a show for his constituents. Six concrete steps and ten feet of sidewalk separated the back door of the building from his parking space, so he could be inside before anyone noticed him.

The elevator dinged a third time and the doors slid open. He liked being on the top floor other than when he had to wait to get out of the building. He stepped inside and pressed the button labeled 1R.

He pulled his phone from his pocket to check for messages from the men working on the funeral arrangements but saw nothing. He shook his head in disappointment when he saw that he had no signal.

"I should get a booster put in this elevator."

As he slid the phone back into his pocket, there was a boom, and the car came to a stop. The LED display said he was on the third floor.

"What is going on, now?" he said and waited to see if it started moving again. It didn't, but the lights flickered once. That was enough to send him to the little box under the floor selector panel where the emergency phone was kept.

He flipped open the door and pulled out the red phone. There was a click and a man's voice answered.

"Johnstown 911. What is your emergency?"

"The back elevator is stuck at City Hall. Get someone over here right now! I have places to be!"

There was a brief silence and the man said, "Hello? Johnstown 911. What is your emergency?"

"Can't you hear me?" Jack screamed into the phone.

"I'm sorry. I can't hear any response, so I am sending an ambulance and fire response to your location now. I show the call is coming from city hall and…"

The phone line went dead with a click and the lights went out in the elevator all at once. Total darkness and silence engulfed the mayor. He pulled his phone from his pocket again and saw that it was off, so he pushed the power button. Nothing happened. It was as if his battery was dead. He never let it get below seventy percent, so that was impossible.

He considered options of what to do. Having seen plenty of action movies, he knew there would have to be an access panel in the ceiling. Getting up to the ceiling and finding the panel in the dark would be a difficult task, though.

As he considered how to do it, he heard a light thump on the roof of the elevator. Then, four heavy footsteps followed. They paced across to the opposite corner and back again. The boom of each step was too loud, but he wrote it off to the absolute silence.

"Hey! Get me out of here!"

There was no response, but he heard something sliding across the metal supports of the roof. Tapping followed and then he heard the emergency panel being pried loose. He stepped to the opposite corner and waited, knowing that he was about to be saved.

The panel gave a screech as if it were bending and then it crashed down into the car. Jack stared, thinking he was glad he moved. A flood light from somewhere up the elevator shaft made a feeble attempt to illuminate the small space.

Jack walked over and looked up, shielding his eyes from the light. He couldn't see his rescuer, but he tried jumping to grab the edge of the opening. It was too high, so he glanced down at the metal handrail that went around the inside of the car.

He tried putting one foot up on the railing to get a boost but couldn't find a handhold. He heard a shuffling sound and looked up to see a gloved hand extended down to him. He pushed himself up with a foot on the railing and grabbed the hand, feeling relieved.

Grabbing onto the edge of the panel opening, he started to pull himself up. He looked to his rescuer with the intent to thank him but saw black orbs where eyes should have been staring back at him out of a badly decomposed face. A horrific grin formed on what was left of the face and Jack let go, falling back into the elevator.

"John Westchester," the thing said in a voice that sounded like a whisper, but filled the car as if it were shouting. "John Westchester."

"No, I'm not John Westchester. I'm Jack. No one calls me John. Who or what are you? Get away from me!"

"John Westchester. The last descendant to bear the name Westchester and you are named John. How fitting."

"Look, I don't know what you want…"

"Oh, I want revenge. I have killed all the others descended from John Westchester that I have found, but you are the prize. You will pay the price just like the others, but now I know the line ends here. That is the cost of his actions."

"I don't know what you're talking about! The fire department is on the way!"

"They'll be much too late," the voice said. Four loud booms followed. It was as if thunder was echoing down the elevator shaft, but it still sounded like footsteps. Jack backed against the wall.

The edge of the ceiling to his right folded in on itself in a sudden jolt. Then, the other side caved in. The mayor let out a scream as the other two edges gave way under what had to be enormous force from above. The sudden movements stopped.

"Someone help! I'm being attacked!"

He heard a deep laugh as the ceiling began to sink. It collapsed as if someone were slowly crushing an aluminum can in their fist. The roof came down enough to prevent Jack from standing up, so he moved to cower in the corner.

"I'll give you anything you want!"

"Good. I want everything!" the voice said. The steel screeched as it folded in further on itself, forcing Jack to the floor. As the wrinkled elevator car crushed him, he screamed in agony, but still heard the thing say, "Revenge is mine."

Chapter 20

Elliott left the detectives outside the coffee shop and went back to the station. She had been working in a conference room in the basement. That had been her choice partially because she needed the space for all the evidence and partially to keep visitors away. Few people went to the basement and that was fine with her.

"There has to be something I'm missing," she said, paging through her notes. "It seems like the mayor is behind it, but that makes no sense. Unless he's a lunatic."

She pondered that while reading four more pages.

"No, he's an ass, but not a lunatic. He's all about money, so killing random people would not help his case. These aren't even people that threaten his plans. They're all relatives, sort of, but no one that could challenge his fortune."

She picked up a stack of photocopies that had been stapled together along the top. Clearly the work of Dr. Cox at the morgue because no one else bound documents like that. It was the log of people who had come in and out of the morgue. Times were meticulously noted, along with the case involved.

It bothered her to see the logs involving all the murders she was trying to solve. So many people had died and she felt that weight on her shoulders every moment she was awake, which ran about twenty-two hours a day.

The mayor had been to the morgue three times a day. Too many times, which made her rethink the lunatic thing. Still, she could attribute it to his eccentricities. Maybe he was worried about how it could affect his development plans, but his focus on the possibility that the remains could be a relative kept coming up over the last couple days.

"Now he has taken the remains, but I can't technically prove that, either. I just need a hint, that's all," she said, continuing to slide her finger along the log. "Wait."

Looking back at the list of murders and then back to the log, she noticed a pattern. It was a weak connection, but still there.

"That's ridiculous. They'll laugh me off the force."

The first few murders happened before the remains were recovered from the well. Four more occurred within the window of time that the coroner was doing her investigation. The reconstruction of the skeleton had taken quite a bit of time. Then, the mayor had gained access to the remains near the time of death for the remaining few. Every murder occurred while the remains were out in the open.

"The skeleton is somehow tied to these killings? I really do need to get more sleep," she said and rubbed her eyes. "It makes absolutely no sense, but until I get a better explanation, I'm going to have to find those remains and seal them up."

Elliott kept a police scanner running on a table near the door while she worked. The calls from the officers going to a murder scene were helpful, but the scanner gave her an advantage. The chatter of traffic stops, and other random activity droned on, but then an anxious voice came through loud and clear.

"All available officers report to City Hall immediately! All officers to City Hall immediately! We have a report of an elevator collapse with possible casualties!" called the dispatcher. She got a sick feeling deep in her stomach and then her phone rang.

"Elliott! It's McEachron!"

"You found the place?"

"We think so. It's in the old flooring shop, down by the ball fields."

"I'm on my way."

"Do we need to respond to city hall?"

"No. You two stay right there. I'm probably going to need you two to clear a path for me. I'm sure the mayor's guy is a big dude."

"He is, but we can handle him."

"Good. Meet me in front of the building when you see me pull up. There's no time to waste," Elliott said and ended the call. She left all her notes on the table, grabbed her keys and raced to the door.

She saw flashing red and blue lights at the crest of the hill on Westchester Road near city hall. Elliott thought Jack was probably dead, but she had to put a stop to this. So, she took a hard right on the road between the coffee and flooring shops. It would have been dramatic for her tires to squeal to a stop, but that's not how things work.

Instead, she killed the engine and jumped out of the car. Schmidt and McEachron ran across the road with weapons drawn. Elliott motioned for them to lead the way. The trio went back along the sidewalk to the computer shop. Schmidt knocked.

"That you, Sal?" called the big man from inside. "Forgot your key again?"

He opened the door and was met with two stun guns pointed at his chest. He put his hands up and grinned, recognizing Schmidt from the window. He shook his head.

"You ladies don't know who you're messing with!" he said.

"We do, actually," Schmidt said. "Now, step back and let us in!"

"You got a warrant?"

"No, but we're coming in, anyway," Elliott said from the back.

"Hey, you're that detective from the news. I better call my boss," he said and slid his hand in his pocket. That was enough for the pair to take the shot. One pair of barbs caught him in the upper, right side of his chest and the other pair embedded in the left side of his pronounced gut.

He yelled out in pain and tried to push through it, but they didn't let up. He stumbled back two steps. Elliott took that opening to slip past him. She threw open the door leading to the flooring shop and saw the funeral setup. The remains from the morgue were on display. Rushing over to the casket, she flipped the liner inside, partially covering the remains. Then, she slammed the lid shut and heard a deep hissing sound.

The lid started opening again, coming up about an inch. She tried pushing it down but realized it didn't latch. She remembered someone telling her that they used a wrench to lock the caskets and glanced around. A ring of Allen wrenches was on a bench along the wall.

She pushed down on the bottom half of the lid and slipped the wrench into the opening, but it was too small. The hissing turned into a rumble, like a storm was forming outside the metal building. She went to the next size up and tried again.

This time, it fit, and she started turning. The other wrenches on the ring made it awkward but she got the first lock set. She then tightened the second one on the bottom half of the lid. When she moved to the top, she found it to be much more challenging. It was as if a person was inside the casket, trying to keep her from closing it.

Schmidt had reloaded her stun gun and was using it to cover the big man on the floor, but he wasn't going anywhere for a while. McEachron saw Elliott struggling and ran over to assist. As Elliott pulled down with all her might, McEachron threw herself on top of the casket. Their combined efforts were enough to close the lid and they heard the rumbling sound turn into a scream. It was a mixture of a man who had just shot himself in the hand and the sound a dog makes when you accidentally step on its foot.

"Hold on!" Elliott yelled over the noise as the wrench slipped into place. She gave five quick twists and then did it again for the other lock. As soon as the wrench stopped turning the room went silent. It was an eerie sensation, and she felt the hairs stand up on the back of her neck.

Elliott let go of the handle and sat back on the red carpet that had been stretched across the concrete floor. McEachron slid down to join her and then Schmidt came in.

"What in the actual hell was that?" she asked, her voice seeming to boom through the now silent storage area.

Chapter 21

"Well, you did it," Zinyemba said as he walked into Elliott's office. He put a steaming cup of coffee on her desk and stepped back to lean against the doorframe. "I'm proud of you."

"Still not a hundred percent sure what I did," she said, as she picked up the drink and blew across the top of it. "I've proofread my notes. I know what it says is what happened, but it's surreal."

"Look. It is the craziest thing I've ever heard of, but somehow you figured it out."

"Yeah, but a lot of people died before I figured it out, including the mayor."

"I'm not sure that's a huge loss for Johnstown."

"Come on now," she said, playfully chastising him. "Jack Westchester has only been dead four days."

"It's his own fault, as far as I can tell! He told them to open that well and that is what unleashed some supernatural entity that killed a whole bunch of people. All of them were related to each other."

"They definitely were, but I guess we'll never know why it happened."

"Unless we open that casket, I suppose."

"Don't even joke about that. Besides, I don't even know where it is right now. Some guys came to the crime scene, shrink-wrapped it, and loaded it in a black panel van. None of them talked to me and I had a call from the chief to turn it over to them without asking questions."

"Crazy stuff," Zinyemba said, sipping his own coffee. "Have you talked to the chief today? He's probably going to want your final report soon."

"He emailed me this morning to say I should meet him in his office at ten o'clock sharp. That's six minutes from now. But, to answer your question, he hasn't said much to me since the mayor was killed. I think he's had his hands full."

"Yeah, I wouldn't want to be in his shoes. Good luck, Red."

"Thanks, Z," she said. The file was in order, so she grabbed it and headed for the door. Zinyemba patted her on the shoulder when she went past him. "Let's grab lunch one of these days. I'm going to go home and pass out after this meeting."

"Just let me know when," he said.

She walked along the corridor. A thick envelope holding her final report was in her left hand and the coffee in her right. Most of the other cops offered a smile or nod, but few said anything. They didn't know all the details per the chief's orders, but they knew she had brought an end to a crime spree of some sort. She knocked once on the chief's door at the end of the hall.

"Come in, Elliott," he said, and she went in, closing the door behind her. "Take a seat."

"Gladly," she said. "I'm exhausted. Here's my final report. Hopefully, it does a better job explaining it than I think it will."

"Yeah, this thing has gotten a lot bigger in the last four days. The mayor went in the ground yesterday and the city council is convening tonight to determine how to proceed. Special elections or appointments or something. More than I want to deal with after these last few weeks."

"I couldn't agree more."

"None of it makes sense to me and, based on what I read of your preliminary report, you don't understand it either. Your story and logic check out, but it doesn't make sense in what I would call reality. I've had calls from people in departments of the government that I've never heard of and hope to never hear of again," he said and took a sip of a brown liquid from a short clear glass. Elliott was confident that was not coffee or tea, probably a well-aged whiskey. She didn't blame him one bit. "Here's what we need to do. We're going to call the case inconclusive, but it's finished."

"But we know…"

"Yes. I agree but hear me out. These are instructions from above my pay grade. Tidy this up to eliminate the supernatural stuff. If it ends up looking like the mayor was behind it, then so be it."

"That's not right," she said with a deep frown. "This is an official document, and I can't just forge it to fit some story. Especially to pin it on an innocent man."

"Not completely innocent, right? He did bring this about."

"He was a greedy fool, but he didn't intend on killing anyone."

"Fine, Elliott. I'm giving you an order. Clean it up and leave it open-ended if you want, but it's done. It can go down as a cold case. I'm sure this thing is over because I believe you solved it. I simply can't jeopardize everything I have waiting for me in retirement by refusing to follow the orders that I've been given. Okay?"

"Yes, sir," she said.

"Look, you can be pissed at me if you want. I'm just telling you what has to be done. No one wants a ghost story tied to this city. It's bad for business or whatever. I'm giving you two weeks off with pay to try and recover from this and to submit your new final report. Take your time."

"I'll have it for you by tomorrow," she said, standing up. She picked up the envelope holding her report, knowing she would have to make some drastic changes to make it match the new narrative.

"You are hard-headed, aren't you?" he said, leaning back in his chair. "Well, things are going to be changing around here. Have a look at that memo in the top tray right there."

She glanced down at a three tiered, black plastic paper tray. She picked up the paper and started reading. It was only three short paragraphs, but she looked up at him as soon as she got to his signature.

"You're quitting?"

"I'm too old for this. I'm worn out and my wife has been pushing me to take the early retirement they've been offering me for two years. I had always hoped I'd go out on top, but surviving to go out is better than nothing."

"Now I feel bad."

"Don't. I would have said all of that if I was in your shoes. You've got a good career ahead of you and I'm willing to bet it will be boring compared to what your first case as detective turned into."

"I can only hope. I really do appreciate you giving me this shot."

"Let's not do this right now. You earned it, just like you've earned a break. Now, go home, get some rest, and I better not hear from you until at least a week from today."

"Yes, sir," she said and offered a salute.

"Get out of here Detective Elliott. I'll see you on the other side."

She didn't like the idea of changing the story behind the case, but she knew some things would always be out of her control. There would be many more cases to solve. The fact she would have a new chief soon bothered her, but she knew that he deserved to move on with life.

Most of the local news outlets had tried reaching her since the case ended, but she refused them all. Everyone knew she had solved the case, and someone would get through to her eventually. She knew it wouldn't be that day. Her phone rang.

"Ugh. Who is this going to be? Restricted. Great. No thanks."

She swiped to ignore the call and slipped it into her pocket. Immediately, the phone started ringing again. Again, the word 'Restricted' showed up, and again she swiped it away. She made it to the car before the third time the phone rang.

"What?" she said.

"Detective Elliott. This is Agent Morales-Rios," the woman at the other end of the call said.

"Who are you and what do you want?"

"We need to have a chat about your case. I'll be at your house in ten minutes."

"No, I'm not meeting any random person who somehow got my phone number to discuss my case."

"I assure you that I am not a random person. I'm an agent with a top level specialized sector of the federal government"

"CIA? FBI?"

"No, but I can't give any more details until we meet in person. I'll be there in nine minutes."

"What do you want?"

"I need to ask you some more questions. We need to fill in more blanks on this case."

"We? What do you do?"

"We deal with things that don't make sense. Your work on the case shows that you are willing to pursue any possibility. That's all I'm at liberty to say over the phone."

"So, you're like Men in Black?"

"Not aliens. Although, the outfit isn't too far off. Please be ready to have a candid conversation that could drastically change the way you think about things. We've already talked to Detective Zinyemba and your chief."

"Alright," Elliott said, and the line went dead. "This day is full of surprises and all I want to do is take a nap."

Chapter 22

  Cousins Charles and John Westchester were both in their late twenties when they pooled what savings they had and bought an eighty-acre tract about twenty miles from the up and coming city of San Luis. While the land wasn't on the main road running west from the city, they believed that the road known then as the Southwestern Trail would be a good place to set up a general store.
  The business wasn't booming, but they had done well enough to have a small house each. Charles lived at the eastern end of their tract and John at the west. Their store was on the other side of the road about half way between their houses. They had planted four small fields on the sloping land below the store and hunted the woods on the acreage behind their homes.
  It was a sunny afternoon with large fluffy clouds in the spring of 1837 when the future of the Westchester plan changed. Charles guided his horse and wagon out onto the trail, turning toward John's house. He glanced to his left down the hill to have a look at a corn field he had planted about a month earlier. He was pleased with its growth.
  He drove past the store, noting that the bottom of one of the shutters had come loose. He'd have to get that fixed after he talked to John. He was confident that his plan would be enough to win over his cousin and then he could think about opening the inn next to the store that they had talked about.
  "Hello!" Charles Westchester said as he walked in through the front door at John's house. The front room held a table with four chairs, a bench with some plain blue cushions, and a cabinet that held a rifle and a shotgun. He could hear John in the back room, which served as the bedroom and had a small porch with a stove on the west side. "John!"

"Yeah, yeah, I'll be right there. You hungry?" John said, carrying a skillet of cornbread into the room. "Just pulled this out of the stove."

"I won't turn down a piece," Charles said with a smile.

"Alright. Give me a minute. I've got some fresh butter."

"That sounds good," Charles said, taking a seat at the table. He flipped over two of the plates stacked at the center of the table and picked a knife from the little tray of silverware. John walked back in with the butter. "I came down to talk business."

"Can we eat first?"

"I have to be over at the store in less than an hour. Mister Joiner is going to be coming by to pick up a roll of barbed wire for his new pasture and I don't want to keep him waiting."

"Fine," John said, cutting into the cornbread.

"You know we've got about twenty-five steady customers. Maybe another ten or fifteen travelers each month. We've been at this for years and it seems like it is going slower than I had hoped."

"We're doing ok. I've saved what I could and I'm hoping to build another room on the back of my house."

"Another room? For what?"

"I've been seeing Scott Patterson's daughter for the last few months, and I think it might be time to get married."

"Whoa, really?"

"I think so. We've been here three years and I'm feeling the desire to get started on a family," John said, scooping out some bread onto Charles' plate and then his own. "Tell me what you wanted to talk about."

"Honestly, it sounds like this talk fits your news pretty well, but I need you to hear me out before you say anything."

"Go ahead," John said before taking a big bite.

"Traffic along the trail here hasn't been what I had thought we'd see. We're staying ahead of repairs on our houses and the store, but not by a lot. I think we've both been counting on side ventures to put any extra aside. You've been going up to the river port to work with your friend, Blaine. His dock seems to be doing well. I've been selling pelts in San Luis to a growing list of customers," he said and took a bite. "The thing is that we are probably making more with those side jobs than with our real plan. So, I'm here to offer to buy your share of our business."

"What?"

"I've been saving up for a year and I think this would be a good move for both of us. I'm offering three hundred and fifty in cash, with a hundred a year for the next three years. That's more than double what we started with. You can keep your house, of course."

"That's generous of you, but I don't want to sell. I think this business can be really good in the long run and obviously we're doing okay if you have that kind of money saved up."

"At least think about it!" Charles said, smacking his hand on the table.

"I tell you what. I'll forgo my back room and make you the same offer! You take the money and I'll pay you another three hundred with the same terms as you gave me."

"That's ridiculous," Charles said. "I'm here to buy you out, not the other way around. I'm not going anywhere."

"Well, too bad, cousin! We're in this together."

"I don't know about that. We barely see each other, except when we cross over at the store. Our lives are getting busy as we pursue the things we want and now you want to go chasing a woman."

"You will speak kindly of her!" John said with a frown.

"Yeah, sure," Charles said, standing and spinning away from the table. He looked out the window to the east at the store. "You've known her for a matter of months and think she's not after your business. Maybe she'd like to meet another Westchester! I could show her more about life than you ever could. I'm the brains behind this whole endeavor and you know it!"

He turned back around to see John standing four feet away. His face was bright red, and he held the skillet up like he would hold an ax, ignoring the pain of the warm metal on his hands. He screamed once and swung, smashing the cast iron skillet into the side of Charles' head.

Charles started to blink his eyes, but the left one wouldn't open. A horrible pain throbbed through his head, and he could taste blood in his mouth. His right eye could see the blue sky and he realized he was outside.

"John..."

His cousin stepped forward and leaned to look down at him.

"John, what are... what are you doing?"

"You crossed the line, cousin. I know you think you're smarter than me, but you're not. I've got more money set back than you can imagine. I've been getting ready for the future. You also told our best customers to keep it a secret that you were buying me out and that big changes were coming."

"I didn't...," Charles said, wincing with the shooting pain.

"Yes, you certainly did," John said. "I hoped it was something we could work through, but I see that isn't possible. You thought you could bully me out, but now you're the one who's out."

Charles tried to bring his hands up to reach out to John, but they were tied together and then down to his feet, which were also bound. He looked up at John again and then at the house, finally putting together that he was lying right next to the well behind the house.

"You're willing to kill for my share of the business? I'll give it to you, and I'll leave. You'll never see me again! Just cut me loose!"

John nodded, "You're laying there with a crushed skull, bleeding all over the place, and you still think I can be tricked. This well is drying up and I've been working on a better one back at the edge of the woods. So, you're right. I'll never see you again."

He grabbed Charles's legs and pulled him to the edge of the well. His cousin tried kicking at him, but only slightly slowed him down. Two mules stood ten feet away in a collar harness, waiting for John's instructions. They were hitched to the large piece of stone that John had shaped to serve as the lid to the well.

"And, Charles, just to show you that I'm smarter than you think. I'll report you missing in a week or so. No one will find any sign of you, and it'll look like you wandered off into the woods. A hunting accident, maybe. The best part is that our business agreement makes me the heir to everything you have, so it will be a quick transition."

"No!" Charles yelled.

"Shut up," John said, and kicked him in the ribs. The force slid him right onto the lip of the well. "A bonus for me is knowing how much you hated going down in those wells at the factory back in the city. Now, you're going to spend eternity in one."

"I underestimated your ruthlessness, but at least I would have had the guts to kill you. You can't even do that," he said through a bloodied smile. "You go make that family but know that this will not go unpunished. Your family will pay for your evil deed."

John offered no response, other than digging the toe of his boot under him and rolling him into the well. He hung up for just a moment and looked down into the darkness. Then, he went in. His head struck the wall twice before he landed in the shallow water at the bottom. In the moments before the pain overtook him, he was able to look up as the mules pulled the stone in place.

THE END